KU-310-920

ADAM SMITH

DEATH CAME CALLING

Complete and Unabridged

LINFORD
Leicester

First published in Great Britain in 2016 by
Robert Hale
an imprint of The Crowood Press
Wiltshire

First Linford Edition
published 2018
by arrangement with
The Crowood Press
Wiltshire

A catalogue record for this book is available
from the British Library.

ISBN 978–1–4448–3946–3

Published by
F. A. Thorpe (Publishing)
Anstey, Leicestershire

Set by Words & Graphics Ltd.
Anstey, Leicestershire
Printed and bound in Great Britain by
T. J. International Ltd., Padstow, Cornwall

This book is printed on acid-free paper

*To Ray Wright and Paul Cairney,
Both sorely missed.*

1

Sheriff Ray Cairney was growing increasingly dissatisfied with the way the town was going.

The newly-formed town council was led by the most influential man Bristow could muster, Curtis Waring. He was also the banker and someone you didn't want to get on the wrong side of, if you valued your business or homestead.

The whole town just reeked of corruption. Not that Ray could put his finger on anything specific — yet.

Taxes were being raised almost monthly because, the town council said Bristow needed to expand and attract investors.

Curtis had heard a rumour emanating in Tucson, that the railroad was planning a spur that would link Bristow to the major cattle markets — as well as

Tucson and neighbouring towns.

Land prices would soar if word got out, and Curtis Waring was going to make sure it didn't.

Council meetings were being held in camera, and the sheriff was not invited, no matter how hard he pushed.

The town council consisted of only four people: Curtis Waring, the banker, as chairman; Ambrose Lowe, rancher; Clint Jenkins, rancher; and Will Lancaster, saloon and hotel owner. All were sworn to secrecy.

Try as he might, Ray couldn't get any information from any of the council members, and this was making him angry. Very angry.

Ray wondered how he was supposed to do his job if he didn't know what was going on.

His anger turned to deep concern when he saw two strangers ride into town.

Under normal circumstances, Ray would have approached the strangers and asked their business, but on this occasion he had a bad feeling about them.

Both were dressed in black with low slung holsters tied to their thighs by leather thongs; a dead giveaway that they were gunnies to be sure.

The two rode to the Silver Dollar saloon, dismounted, tied their mounts to the hitch rail and entered.

Sure would like to be a fly on the wall right now, Ray thought as he ambled across the street towards the saloon.

He didn't enter; he walked slowly past looking through each of the six small windows, three set either side of the batwings which gave him a good view of the interior.

The strangers were at the far end of the bar and, as Ray reached the last window, he saw Will Lancaster coming out of his private office and heading towards the two men.

Ray turned and walked back past the saloon. As he did, he saw Lancaster shake the hands of the two men and usher them into his office.

Well, well, Ray thought. *What the hell's going on? Why has Lancaster sent for two hard cases?*

Ray walked back across the street and rolled himself a cigarette. There was a rocking chair outside the general store which was opposite the saloon. He sat down and lit up, waiting to see what, if anything, developed.

He didn't have to wait long.

Swampy, the general dogsbody of the saloon, came running through the batwings and headed uptown.

Just as he finished his smoke, Curtis Waring appeared and walked straight into the saloon.

No sooner had Waring gone in than Clint Jenkins arrived, quickly followed by Ambrose Lowe.

Swampy was the last to arrive and he seemed out of breath as he ambled along the sidewalk.

So it's not just Lancaster, Ray thought, *the town council have hired them — or are trying to!*

Ray's brain was buzzing. Something

4

was going down, of that he was certain. But what? He'd get no help from the town council — that was for sure!

For the life of him, Sheriff Ray Cairney could think of no reason for gunslingers to be in Bristow.

Apart for the usual drunken brawls on Saturday nights, there'd been no gunplay for as long as Ray could remember. No robberies. No land disputes that he was aware of. Nothing. Bristow was a most peaceful — and safe — place to live.

Thirty minutes after the town council members had entered the Silver Dollar, they began to leave. One at a time at five minute intervals.

Obviously, they didn't want to raise suspicion, Ray thought. But what were they hatching?

Ray decided he'd get himself a beer, and maybe buy one for Swampy, too.

' 'Evenin', Sheriff. What'll it be?' the barkeep asked.

'Beer, Charlie. Make it two,' Ray said.

'Comin' up, Sheriff.'

Swampy was doing what he always did: collecting glasses and, if he was lucky, draining the dregs of whatever was in the glass.

'Beer here for you, Swampy,' the sheriff called out.

Swampy's face lit up like a baby that has found some candy.

Ray took the beers from the bar top and walked to a secluded table. He didn't want his conversation overheard by the barman who was a renowned gossip.

Ray sat at a table and watched Swampy shuffle across to join him. Already Swampy was licking his lips in anticipation of a fresh beer.

He flopped into a chair and, thanking the sheriff, without looking at him, Swampy stared at the beer.

'Go ahead, Swampy, it's yours,' Ray said, a slight grin on his face.

Without taking his eyes off the beer pot, Swampy picked the glass up and drank. He drank in one go until the glass was empty.

Ray signalled the barkeep for another beer. 'Busy day today, Swampy?'

'No more'n usual,' Swampy replied. 'Appreciate the beer, Sheriff.'

'Saw you scooting down the street earlier.'

'Yeah, had to get some fellas to meet up with Mr Lancaster,' Swampy replied, all the time looking at the barkeep, waiting for his beer.

'Saw two fellas arrive earlier,' Ray said, trying not to make it obvious he was fishing.

Swampy's second beer arrived but, before he could pick it up, Ray put his hand over the glass.

'Know who they are?'

'Nope. But they sure look like mean critters to me,' Swampy said, never taking his eyes off the glass of beer.

'Tell you what,' Ray said, 'you hear anythin', an' I mean *anythin*, you let me know. There'll be beer as a reward.'

Swampy's face lit up. 'Sure, Sheriff, I'll do that!'

Ray took his hand off the beer glass and instantly, Swampy picked it up in case the sheriff changed his mind.

Ray drank half his beer and stood up. 'Don't forget now. You hear anything, no matter how small, you tell me, OK?'

'I won't forget, Sheriff, and mighty thanks for the beers.'

Ray left the saloon and headed back to his office.

2

The conversation between the sheriff and Swampy hadn't gone unnoticed.

By chance, Will Lancaster came out of his office to check on the takings, but he stopped in the doorway, looking at the sheriff and Swampy.

He didn't like what he saw, not one bit.

He couldn't hear what was being said but no one ever bought Swampy a drink. No one. The sheriff was obviously fishing for information about the two strangers.

Lancaster backed into his office and closed the door.

'We may have a problem,' he said.

The two strangers, Chad and Burt Slim, brothers, showed no emotion whatsoever at this statement.

'The sheriff has been nosing around. Just seen him buying drinks for

Swampy. That can mean only one thing: he's bribing Swampy for information.'

Lancaster paused, looking from one man to the other. The brothers looked once at each other before Chad asked, 'What do you want us to do?'

'Well, I don't think killing the sheriff is a good idea, that would bring the county marshal here and he'd start sniffing around.'

'So it's Swampy then,' Burt said. 'We'll settle this after dark. You send him on an errand at ten o'clock.'

Lancaster mopped his brow. This was more than he'd bargained for in going in with Waring, Jenkins and Lowe, but it was too late to pull out now. Besides, the lure of the expected profits to be made when Waring started to foreclose on the homesteads and ranches in the path the railroad was likely to take was too great to ignore.

★　★　★

At five before ten that same evening, Will Lancaster sent for Swampy.

'Go check my buggy, will you? I think I left a saddle bag in it. It's at the rear of the livery.' Lancaster said all this without once looking into the eyes of Swampy.

Despite the old man being an alcoholic, dirty and smelly, Lancaster had always had a soft spot for him and what he was about to cause grated. But he knew it had to be done.

'Sure thing, Mr Lancaster, sir. Be right back.'

Swampy left the office and Lancaster took a deep breath before going to the drinks cabinet and taking out a bottle of fine French brandy. He settled back behind his desk, opened the bottle and poured a more than generous amount into a crystal brandy glass.

He sat for several minutes, swirling the amber liquid around the glass, his mind in a turmoil of guilt.

He took a mouthful of brandy, put the glass down and lit a cigar.

11

Somehow, the combination of brandy and a cigar soothed him — that and the thought of riches to come. Slowly, he was able to dismiss Swampy from his mind, and justify what was about to happen.

Cold blooded murder.

* * *

There were several street lanterns along Main Street, but none at all down the various side alleys. Swampy reached the livery stable, which was deserted at this time of night, and turned into the alley that led to the corral at the rear.

Chad and Burt Slim had already positioned themselves in the dark alley. One to the left and one to the right.

As Swampy reached their position, Burt called out, 'Hey, Swampy, where you off to?'

As Swampy turned towards the sound of the voice, one he did not recognize, Chad came up behind him and before Swampy could react, a

Bowie knife sliced through his throat, almost ear to ear.

For seconds, Swampy felt nothing as blood spurted from his neck, then realization dawned in his befuddled brain as his legs gave way and he sagged, rather than fell, to the ground, both hands gripping his throat in a futile effort to staunch the flow of blood.

He then fell forwards, hitting the dirt face down. For a few moments his legs twitched as blood gurgled from his throat.

Then he stopped moving.

Chad stepped forward and wiped the blade of the Bowie on Swampy's back, and returned it to its sheath. They dragged Swampy's body to the side of the alley. Then both men headed back to the saloon.

They entered at the rear so as not to be seen and went straight to Lancaster's office. They walked in without knocking, making Lancaster jump, spilling brandy on his blotter.

The Slim brothers did not utter a word, but Chad, seeing the brandy, picked it up and drank straight from the bottle then passed it to Burt, who did the same.

'Is it . . . have you . . . ?'

'You'll need a new dogsbody,' was all he got in response to his almost unasked question.

Lancaster drained his glass, his hands visibly shaking.

'You got our rooms ready?' Burt asked.

'What? Oh, er, yes. Numbers 1 and 2, top of the stairs on the left facing Main Street. Keys are in the doors.' Lancaster was breathing heavily at the thought of the now dead Swampy. 'What did you do with, er, you know . . . ' he added.

'Left him in the alley,' Chad said.

'Oh.' Lancaster poured another brandy and gulped it down. It didn't completely alleviate his deep feeling of guilt, but it did deaden it somewhat.

The Slim brothers left the room without saying a word.

Lancaster flopped back in his chair and put his head in his hands.

★ ★ ★

At 7 a.m. every morning, Sheriff Ray Cairney began his morning rounds — being a creature of habit, you could set your watch by him.

He often varied the route, but he made sure he checked the doors of every store — including the saloon. The last place he always checked was the livery. Old Sam would already be there with the coffee brewing and they'd do their usual ritual of a coffee, cigarette and a chat.

'Morning, Sam.'

'Morning, Sheriff. Coffee?' Sam asked.

'You need to ask?' Ray replied, smiling.

'Coming right up.'

Ray sat on a barrel and took his makings out. The first cigarette of the day was always the best; it was downhill thereafter.

'You get a look at them two strangers that came into town yesterday?' Ray asked, licking his cigarette paper.

'Sure did. Mean looking dudes too, if'n you ask me,' Sam replied, bringing over two tin mugs of Arbuckle's finest.

'Recognize 'em?'

'Nope. They ain't never been here afore. They plain scared the cahoolies outta me. Eyes like black stones.'

'They say anything?'

'Asked how much for feed and groom for a week. I told 'em, added a bit on, and they handed over the money saying, 'You better take care of 'em good', and left.'

After a moment's pause, Ray asked, 'Notice anythin' about them?'

'Well, apart from their low-slung Colts and a Bowie knife and two of the latest Winchester repeaters, they looked as if they'd ridden in hell — and won!' Sam took a sip of his coffee, before lighting his pipe.

Puffing out a cloud of blue smoke, Sam coughed, spat and added, 'Two of

16

the deadliest hombres I ever did see.'

Ray was silent. He drained his coffee and stomped out his cigarette butt.

'Well, think I'll take another look round. See you tomorrow, Sam.'

'Take care, Sheriff. Coffee'll be ready.' Sam did what passed for a grin and gave a brief wave.

Outside, the air was still refreshingly cool. Ray knew as the day wore on the temperature would rise and by mid-afternoon, the heat would be stifling.

For Ray, this was the best part of the day. Cool breeze, and only a handful of people about, getting their stores ready for whatever the day might bring.

So content was Ray that he almost didn't see the pile of rags piled on the right side of the alley.

He sighed deeply; one of his pet hates was people dumping their trash any-where they felt like it. As he neared the pile, he suddenly saw it was not rags, but a man.

'Jeez!' was all Ray could say. He knelt down beside the body and turned it over. 'Swampy! Dear God!'

He looked at the distorted features of the old man and a tear crept unbidden from one eye.

In a blinding flash, the sheriff realized that he'd been killed for talking to him the previous night. Could be no other reason. The old man, if not universally liked, was nevertheless a character, and had no enemies that Ray could think of. He was just a harmless old man.

Ray got himself together and reviewed the events of yesterday: two hard cases ride in, go straight to the saloon. Swampy comes running out to fetch Waring, Jenkins and Lowe, and they all turn up within ten minutes.

After a short meeting, which Ray knew the hard cases were a part of, they all went their ways — except the gunnies.

Coincidence? Ray didn't think so.

At the end of the alley, at Main Street, one or two people had stopped. They were soon joined by half a dozen more.

'He dead, Sheriff?' one of them called out.

'Yeah. He's dead. Throat cut. Someone get the undertaker, pronto.' Ray was still crouching over the body, one hand on the old man's shoulder.

'Who is it?' another voice called.

Ray didn't answer straightaway. Then, after taking a deep breath; he didn't want his voice to sound as shaky as he felt, he said, 'It's ol' Swampy.'

There was a collective murmur of both surprise and shock. 'Who the hell would want to kill ol' Swampy? He never did no one no harm, sure he was smelly an' always on the cadge but . . . ' The man stopped, sighed and shook his head.

At that moment the undertaker, Ethan Doom arrived, dressed all in black — as usual — and the crowd parted to let his wagon through.

'Who — ' Ethan stopped as he recognized the dead man and saw the gash across his neck. 'Goddamn! Who would do such a thing?'

'I don't know, but I'm sure gonna find out,' the sheriff replied.

Ethan lifted the coffin from the wagon and placed it on the ground beside Swampy.

'I'll give you a hand,' Ray said.

'I don't like to bring it up, Sheriff, but ol' Swampy weren't no rich man. Who's gonna pay for the coffin and funeral?'

'Don't worry about that, Ethan. I'll take care of it, just send me the bill,' Ray said as he helped lift the body into the coffin.

Ethan arranged Swampy's arms across his chest and placed the coffin lid on.

'I won't nail it down yet,' Ethan said. I'll clean him up some. I got plenty of old clothes back at the shop. He'll get a decent burial.'

'Thanks, Ethan, 'preciate that.'

They loaded the coffin on to the wagon and, slowly, Ethan set off.

3

Sheriff Cairney walked back to his office with leaden feet. He knew, but could not prove yet, who the killers were. He also knew that he'd made a mistake in talking to Swampy in the saloon.

They killed Swampy for what they thought he might know.

Fact was, the poor old man knew nothing! He'd been killed for *nothing*.

He filled his mug with stale, lukewarm coffee and flopped down in his chair. Slowly, he rolled a cigarette, lit it and inhaled deeply.

He needed a deputy. If he was to investigate what was going down in Bristow, it would be a full-time job, he'd need someone to do the mundane tasks around the town: doing the rounds first thing in the morning and last thing at night; sorting out the

21

occasional drunk and generally taking care of any disputes that might arise.

Ray decided to see Waring and insist they hired a deputy. Ray already had a man in mind, Otis Culver.

At the moment, Otis worked as an odd-job man, usually helping out Sam at the livery, doing the heavy stuff Sam could no longer do.

Ray drained his coffee and grimaced at the bitter taste. 'Sure hope he can make better coffee than I can,' he said out loud.

Stubbing out his half-smoked cigarette, he donned his Stetson and set off for the bank.

*　*　*

Ambrose Lowe, the rancher and town council member, had just heard through the grapevine of Swampy's murder. He wasted no time in riding into town to see Will Lancaster and find out what the hell was going on. He tied his horse to the hitch rail and burst through the batwings.

'Where's Will?' he asked the barkeep.

'In his office, Mr Lowe,' the 'keep replied. 'Shall I tell him you're here?'

'No. I'll go in.'

'I b'lieve he's busy, sir. Better that I — '

But Ambrose Lowe ignored the 'keep and stormed into Lancaster's office.

Lancaster looked up.

'Ambrose, I'm kinda busy right now, if you — '

'What the hell is going on? I just heard about Swampy. Those two goons do it?'

'I don't know what — '

'Don't lie to me, Lancaster. Why was old Swampy murdered?'

Lancaster took a deep breath and sighed. 'Sheriff Cairney was in here yesterday, he bought Swampy a coupla beers and they sat and had a cosy chat in the saloon.'

'An' you had him killed for that?' Lowe was beside himself with fury. 'You dang fool, Lancaster. Don't you think the sheriff will put two and two together?'

'I was just trying to safeguard the operation.' Lancaster's voice was more like a whine.

'Safeguard! Goddammit to hell, you just highlighted it.'

'I didn't think it — '

'You didn't think at all!' Lowe shouted at him. 'The sheriff is going to be crawling all over us from now on.'

'I can vouch the Slim brothers never left my office,' Lancaster began.

'An' you think that'll satisfy the sheriff? You're a fool, Lancaster. From now on you do nothing without consulting us first. *Is that clear*?'

Lancaster's hang-dog expression told Lowe that it was perfectly clear.

Ambrose Lowe stormed out of the office, slamming the door loudly.

Little did he know that the barkeep, Charlie Yates, had positioned himself at the far end of the bar which was adjacent to Lancaster's office. Ambrose Lowe's voice was loud. Very loud.

Although he couldn't hear Lancaster's replies, he heard enough to work out what was going on. And, more importantly, who had killed Swampy.

★   ★   ★

Sheriff Cairney entered the bank and walked up to the head cashier. A snooty fellow with ideas above his station.

'I want to see Waring,' he demanded.

I'm afraid *Mr* Waring is busy, Sheriff,' the cashier replied, looking down his nose.

'Then *un*busy him. Now!'

The look on the sheriff's face was enough to make the chief cashier almost jump to obey his demand.

He returned in less than a minute. 'Mr Waring will see you now, Sheriff.'

Ray didn't respond, he strode to the manager's office and, without knocking, entered.

'Sheriff, good to see you. What can I do for you?' Waring said cheerily.

'What you can do is tell me what the

hell is going on,' the sheriff said.

'Why? I don't know what you mean,' Waring said guardedly.

'Why'd you hire those two gunslingers?' the sheriff asked.

'That is of no concern of yours, Sheriff.' Waring's tone had changed.

'It is when there's murder involved,' the sheriff spat.

'Surely, Sheriff, you don't think they had anything to do with the killing of Swampy,' Waring said in a dismissive tone.

'Mighty big coincidence, don't you think? They ride into town and a matter of hours later, Bristow has its first killing for over three years.' The sheriff was standing with his arms folded across his chest.

'You're adding two and two and getting five, Sheriff,' Waring said.

'I know one thing. You and your cronies are up to something, an' I aim to find out what it is. I'm warning you now, I'll be watching you very carefully.'

'I'd be very careful if I was you,

Sheriff,' Waring said.

'Are you threatening the law?' Ray rested his right hand on the butt of his holstered Colt. 'Cos in my book, I could lock you up for that.'

'Not a threat, Sheriff. A piece of advice.' Waring leaned back in his chair, an acerbic smile on his face. 'Now, if you'll excuse me, I have the small matter of running a bank — and a town!'

'I'm taking on Otis Culver as my deputy; any objections?' Ray said.

Waring felt he needed to placate the sheriff, so he agreed. 'Give him a month's trial,' he said.

Ray left the office without a word but, instead of slamming the door, he left it wide open, knowing this would irritate Waring.

* * *

The sheriff's next port of call was the Silver Dollar and Will Lancaster.

Lancaster had turned up in Bristow almost six years ago and established himself pretty damn quickly. He bought the Silver Dollar with cash — paying a tad over the odds, so the story went.

No one knew where he'd come from or how he'd made his money, but after the opening night of the Silver Dollar, with free food and drinks, no one cared about his background.

He was a larger than life character, with a booming voice and a laugh that was infectious. Lancaster was one of the most popular men in Bristow.

Standing a little over six feet tall with a belly that showed a good life, he sported a walrus moustache and always seemed to be smiling.

Except today, he wasn't.

When Sheriff Cairney entered Lancaster's office without knocking; he saw a man slumped forward on his desk, slightly the worse for drink.

'Need a word, Will,' Ray said.

Slowly, Lancaster lifted his head, his bloodshot eyes gradually focusing on the sheriff.

'Jeez, man. You look as if you've been

here all night!' Ray said.

Lancaster sat upright. His clothes were crumpled and stained, totally out of character for a man who prided himself on his appearance.

'You don't look too good, Will,' the sheriff said.

Lancaster picked up his nearly empty brandy glass, his hand shaking as he drained it.

'What do you know about Swampy's murder?' Ray asked. He could see the effect the question had on Lancaster.

'I . . . I . . . what makes you think I know . . . anything?' Lancaster replied, his voice shaky and his face drained of blood.

Before Ray could respond, their meeting was brought to an abrupt halt.

Four shots were heard, and they came from the saloon.

Ray drew his Colt immediately, wishing, at the same time, he'd brought the scattergun with him.

Opening the office door cautiously, Ray stepped into the now silent saloon bar. Men were just standing and crouching, staring at the bodies of two rannies, laid out in a rapidly growing pool of blood.

'What the hell — ' Ray began.

Burt Slim, leaning on the bar, glass of beer in one hand said, 'They drew on us, Sheriff. It was a fair fight, ask anyone.'

'That right, Charlie?' Ray asked the barkeep.

Charlie looked a little sheepish, but told the story.

'Rory and Calhoun, there, they accused these two — er — gentlemen of killin' ol' Swampy. When they denied it, Rory went for his gun, calling them damn liars. Calhoun was seconds behind him, but, hell, they ain't — weren't no gunslingers.

'They loosed off a shot each, but missed by a country mile. These two drew and shot and, well, you can see the result.' Charlie stopped, his head low. The two dead men had been pals of his.

'I'll need you two to come down to the office, I want a statement, so's it's properly recorded in law.' Ray holstered his Colt and pointed to the batwings. 'After you,' he said.

Burt Slim drained his beer and, followed by his brother, they left the saloon.

The three men entered the sheriff's office and Ray took out two sheets of paper and two pencils.

'OK, in your own words. I assume you can write?' Ray added laconically.

'We can read, too,' Chad said, speaking for the first time.

Ray sat behind his desk and watched as the two men started to write.

'So,' Ray asked, 'what brings you to Bristow?'

'Jus' passing through, Sheriff,' Burt said without looking up.

'You seem to know Will Lancaster quite well,' Ray stated.

'Nope. Only jus' met him.'

'What about the other council members — you ever met them before?'

31

'Nope.'

'Hmm,' was all Ray said.

The Slim brothers finished writing their statements and stood to leave.

'I'll be watching you, boys,' Ray said.

'Watch away, Sheriff,' Burt said and the two men left the office.

Ray read and reread both statements. They were almost identical. Each man had signed the bottom and Ray added his signature before filing them away.

He was more convinced than ever that the Slim brothers had murdered Swampy.

Now he had to prove it!

★ ★ ★

'Otis, you got a minute?' Ray asked, as Otis came out of the hay loft at the livery.

'Sure thing, Sheriff. Be right down.'

'Got a job for you,' Ray said.

A beaming smile lit up Otis's face.

'How would you like to be my deputy? Month's trial, and if it works out, a permanent one.' Ray didn't think Otis's smile could get any bigger. But it did.

'Hot damn!' Otis was jumping with delight. 'Hot damn!' was all he could say.

'I take it that's a yes?'

'You bet it's a 'yes'! When do I start?'

'Don't you want to know the wage and the hours?' Ray said.

'I'll work all day every day an' I'd do it for free,' Otis said, the smile still on his face, making him look even younger than he was.

'No need fer that,' Ray said, smiling at the boy's enthusiasm. 'Report to the office first thing and I'll swear you in and give you your badge of office. You get thirty a month, food and a supply of ammo. You got a gun?'

'Sort of, it's pretty old and not reliable.' Otis hung his head as if he thought the offer might be withdrawn.

'Get over to Cy's, tell him you need a .45, and gun belt and holster and to bill the council. We got two scatterguns and four Winchesters, so you've no need to get a rifle. OK?'

Again, Otis beamed. 'Yes, sir, Sheriff.'

'Call me Sheriff in public, but Ray when we ain't.'

'Yes, sir, Sheriff — I mean, Ray.'

'See you in the morning.' The two men shook hands and Ray went back to the office. His next job was to go through the mountain of Wanted notices and hope the Slim brothers were there.

★ ★ ★

Curtis Waring was a worried man. There was no way he was going to let the sheriff ruin his carefully laid plans. OK, he thought, I made a mistake in sending for the Slim brothers, but we need a couple of 'slingers to back us up.

In his mind, Waring was justifying his actions, all he had to do now was convince the others. In particular, Will Lancaster, as Waring believed him to be the weak link in the operation.

34

He went to the door and called for young Alfred, the messenger boy and told him to ride out to Ambrose Lowe and Clint Jenkins and give them a message: *Meeting here tonight, ten o'clock. Tell them to use the rear entrance. Take the buggy, it's at the livery, and I'd like you to stay here this evening, to let them in, Alfred. You'll be well compensated.*

'Yes, sir. I'll leave straight away.' With that Alfred almost ran out of the office, so eager was he to impress.

Waring decided he would see Lancaster personally.

He settled back behind his desk, content that he'd made a decision.

'A whiskey, I think,' he said out loud, and walked to the drinks cabinet, unlocked it and took out a bottle of rye and a crystal tumbler. He was about to pour when he had a better idea.

'The good stuff, I think,' he said to himself.

He put the rye back in the cabinet and took out a bottle of single malt whiskey. This was reserved for 'special' clients, and by that, he meant rich ones.

He poured himself a generous measure, placed the bottle back in the cabinet — and locked it.

Sitting once more behind his expensive mahogany desk, Waring savoured every mouthful of the single malt, taking small sips and swirling the liquid round his mouth before swallowing.

Draining the last delicious drop, he reached for his hat and set off for the Silver Dollar.

* * *

Ray was still in his office, going through the Wanted notices, hoping to find what he was looking for. So far, and nearly three-quarters of the way through the pile, he'd found nothing. Ray's methodical brain and endless patience meant he wouldn't give up till he'd looked at every single notice.

The day wore on, the sun's heat was stifling and, by late afternoon, heat haze was rising from the ground, adding to his discomfiture.

He decided to take a break; maybe he'd get a cool beer over at the saloon and see what gossip was doing the rounds.

By sheer chance, as Ray opened the office door, Waring marched past on the opposite side of Main Street.

'Well, well,' Ray said aloud, 'seems I've caused some ripples.' He watched as Waring turned left into the side alley of the saloon. Obviously, Ray thought, he was going to use the rear entrance. Another clandestine meeting.

Ray walked quickly to the saloon and entered through the batwings just in time to see Waring disappear into Lancaster's office.

Charlie, the barkeep, was at the far end of the bar, trying to look busy by polishing some glasses that didn't need polishing. Ray grinned. Earwigging, he thought.

'A beer please, Charlie,' Ray said.

'Comin' right up,' Charlie said, but it was obvious he didn't really want to leave his listening post.

The beer came remarkably quickly, and Ray couldn't help but grin. 'Anything interestin'?' He asked.

Without batting an eye, Charlie said, 'Nah, talking low, cain't make out a word. Not like this morning', when ol' Ambrose was here, shoutin' and cursin' fit to make the Devil blush.'

'Anything I should know about?' Ray said.

'Not here, Sheriff, and not now. I sure don't wanna end up like poor ol' Swampy.'

Ray felt his stomach lurch at that remark, but understood. 'When then, Charlie?'

'After sunset, late on, I'll come to your back door and knock three times, so's you know it's me. OK?'

'OK.'

* * *

The conversation between Lancaster and Waring was indeed quiet. Waring

38

was doing most of the talking, telling Lancaster, in no uncertain terms, that their plan must go ahead. The foreclosure notices were ready and, with Chad and Burt Slim, they had enforcers to make sure the small ranch owners and homesteaders left with little fuss.

'You just don't get it, do you, Will? It's a simple and foolproof plan. The bank forecloses on property and sells it at market rate, which at the moment is $2–3 an acre. You, Ambrose and Clint buy the land at that price.

'The bank gets its money back and, when the railroad spur is announced, that same land will be worth anything from $10–12 an acre!'

Waring paused to let this sink in.

'The railroad will require between 20,000 to 30,000 acres, so let's take the lower figure of twenty. Now, at the top price of $3 an acre, that's an outlay of $60,000.

'Let's take the lower selling price of $10 an acre, that's a total of $200,000.

Giving us a profit of $140,000, split four ways.'

Again, Waring paused.

When Lancaster didn't respond with anything, Waring continued. 'But the plan is not to split the money. The plan is to buy this town, lock, stock and barrel. Have you any idea how much money we could make?'

Lancaster shook his head wearily.

'Millions! We can make millions. What we *don't* need is a weak link. And at the moment, that weak link is you, Will, you.

'The first eviction takes place tonight. I'm sending Burt and Chad to serve notice on the Higgins' place. It's 4,000 acres, which Ambrose will buy from my bank tomorrow. Now, you're either with us, or agenst us. What is it to be?'

The silence that followed the question seemed to drag on forever until Lancaster looked up for the first time and spoke.

'I don't want any more killing,' was all he said.

'I take it that's a yes, then?' Waring said with a forced grin on his face.

'No more killing,' Lancaster repeated.

'Swampy was, er, unfortunate. It was necessary to safeguard our plan. We couldn't have him blabbing all over town now, could we?' Waring stood and helped himself to a drink.

'He didn't know a thing,' Lancaster said. 'And even if he did, he would've forgotten it by the next drink.'

'We couldn't take that chance. Our ever-vigilant sheriff was on his case. It was our opinion that the sheriff had told Swampy to report anything he heard.' Waring took a sip of his brandy and studied Lancaster's face.

'There's a meeting tonight, ten o'clock at the bank, it'll be good and dark by then. Use the rear entrance and make sure you ain't seen by anyone, particularly the sheriff.' Lancaster drained his glass and stood up. He pulled his vest down over his ample stomach and adjusted his frock coat. 'I'll see you then. And smarten yourself up.'

4

Ray had thoroughly searched through the mountain of Wanted posters and hadn't found any that resembled the Slim brothers.

Frustrated, he filled the coffee pot and placed it on the wood stove. He was so sure he'd find something, anything that, in law, meant he could arrest the brothers.

With no help from the so-called town council, he knew he was on his own. Unless someone slipped up somehow, but how? Ray didn't even know what he was looking for — except to prove that the brothers had killed Swampy.

But what were they hiding?

His thoughts were interrupted by three knocks on the back door. Charlie! Ray had almost forgotten about him.

Opening the door he ushered Charlie in. 'I just put some fresh coffee on,' Ray said, walking towards the office.

'I reckon not goin' in there,' Charlie said. 'Too many passersby.'

'OK, the cells are empty, I'll bring the coffee through.'

Charlie, as nervous as a prairie dog, entered the first cell. Ray was back within a minute with the coffee pot and two tin mugs. He set the mugs down on the empty cot and poured the steaming liquid into them.

He wasn't going to push Charlie, so he waited for the man to speak.

'I don't know how important this stuff is, but I heard Ambrose Lowe shouting at Will Lancaster over some-thing that Will had done, or had *had* done, that didn't sit well with Ambrose.'

'What exactly did you hear?' Ray asked, sipping at the hot coffee.

'Well, there were no names men-tioned that I heard, but Ambrose said, 'You had him killed for that!' Just thought you should know, Sheriff.'

Charlie drained his coffee and said, 'I best be away now.'

'Thanks for the information, Charlie, you take care. An' if you hear anything else . . . '

'Sure thing, Sheriff,' Charlie said and scuttled out the back door.

* * *

It was just on eight o'clock that night when Ray decided to do the rounds. Bristow had mostly closed down for the night. All the stores were closed and bathed in the eerie blue light of a full moon. The exception, of course, was the Silver Dollar.

A row of lanterns hung over the boardwalk, and another row hung inside; it attracted customers like moths to a flame.

Although business was pretty steady throughout the day, the busiest time was always between eight and ten at night. That was when Lancaster made his money.

The saloon was packed with ranch hands from the surrounding ranches, as

44

well as a few townsfolk, and shop-keepers having a quick one or two before going home. At weekends during the season, when the cattle drives came through, there was a rougher element filling the saloon. Men who drank as much as their bellies could handle — it could be another six weeks before they got another drink.

Ray took his usual route around town, checking doors and windows, tipping his hat at the few people on their way home or to the saloon. Apart from the tinkle of the out-of-tune piano played by anyone who fancied it, the town was quiet. Just the way Ray liked it.

There'd be a few drunks later on, that was almost guaranteed, but rarely was there any trouble that he couldn't handle.

At around 9.30, Ray went to the café to pick up his evening meal — usually a stew of some kind, but now and then a steak and eggs. He took the plate back to his office, put some coffee on and retrieved the bottle of bourbon he kept in the bottom drawer of his desk. A creature of habit, he always had a coffee spiked with a measure of bourbon while he ate.

Although he had a room in the hotel, paid for by the town council, he spent most nights on a cot in the cells, the only exception being if the cells were full of drunks sleeping it off.

Fortunately, that didn't happen often.

Ray sat at his desk and took the cover off his meal — it was stew, with two hunks of bread already soaked in gravy.

The office filled with the aroma of the beef stew and the near-boiling coffee and Ray ate with relish.

Just as Ray was mopping up the last of the stew with a hunk of bread, he happened to glance up and look out of the office window in time to see a furtive Ambrose Lowe cut down the alleyway by the side of the bank.

Two minutes later, Clint Jenkins did the same thing. Ray sipped on his bourbon coffee and waited to see if Will

Lancaster followed on.

He wasn't disappointed. If ever three men could look so guilty just walking down the street, Ray thought, he'd just seen them.

The sheriff turned the lamp down real low and stepped towards the window to get a better view. He just caught sight of Lancaster entering the bank by the rear door.

'So,' Ray said out loud, 'another secret council meeting!'

After twenty minutes, Ray was about to give up when to his surprise, he saw the Slim brothers leave the bank.

'Now where the hell are they going?'

The two men turned left and Ray guessed they were heading for the livery stable. But to go where? A few moments later two horsemen rode down Main Street, heading north.

Ray was beginning to wish he'd started Otis straightaway instead of the next day. He couldn't be in two places at once.

The sheriff was trying to decide

whether to follow the Slim brothers or wait for the meeting to end and tackle Will Lancaster. He was still undecided when he saw Ambrose Lowe make a furtive exit from the rear of the bank.

Ray made up his mind to wait for Lancaster.

It was another ten minutes before Clint Jenkins appeared in the alley and a further fifteen minutes before Lancaster appeared.

Lancaster was nervous. Very nervous. When he reached the end of the alley, he stopped and, holding on to a building for support, he peeked into Main Street, looking left and then right. He hesitated for a few more seconds before he stepped up on to the boardwalk and scuttled towards the saloon.

It seemed to Ray that Lancaster was trying to look in all directions at once and in his nervousness, he broke into a lumbering trot.

Ray watched him until he was out of sight, then he left the office to confront him in the saloon.

The light wind was still warm and strong enough to lift sand off Main Street, forming small dust devils.

Ray kept to the boardwalk on the opposite side of the street, but he could no longer see Will Lancaster. The Silver Dollar was around a hundred yards away and Ray felt certain that, even trotting, Lancaster wouldn't have reached it yet.

Ray cautiously crossed the street, his right hand resting on the butt of his Colt.

Did Will duck down an alley? And if so, why?

There were two side alleys before you reached the Silver Dollar. Neither of them was lit, and what little light coming from the moon was blocked by the buildings.

Ray stood to one side of the first alley and cautiously peered into the bleak blackness in the hope of something catching his eye. The town seemed ominously quiet; even the out-of-tune piano in the saloon had stopped playing and the atmosphere was heavy. Ray wasn't sure whether it was just in his mind, but the hairs on the back of his head bristled and a shiver went down his spine.

With his Colt now firmly held in his right hand and his eyes becoming used to the darkness, Ray edged into the alley. His senses heightened as he stared into the gloom with eyes as wide as possible, looking for any movement, his ears listening for the slightest sound.

At the far end of the alley, the moon's silver grey light suddenly appeared. Ray tensed. His finger rested lightly on the trigger, ready to shoot in a split second if need be.

He took another three tentative steps down the alley and that's when he saw a lump on the ground, propped up against the side of a building. There was a small, flickering light emanating from it and, as Ray drew closer, he saw it was a tie-pin reflecting what little light there was.

Ray knelt beside the body.

The body of Will Lancaster.

Futilely, he felt for a pulse. Of course, there wasn't one.

Ray reached into his vest pocket and ignited a match. The flickering flame illuminated a face frozen in shock and a neck that had been slit from ear to ear.

Ray whirled round as the sound of hoof-beats thundered down Main Street. He ran to the end of the alley, but only caught a brief glimpse of two horses before the night swallowed them up.

'Goddamn!' Ray shouted. 'Goddamn!' He had no doubt as to the identity of the riders.

Ray holstered his pistol, took off his Stetson and wiped the head band with a bandanna. He hadn't realized how much he'd been sweating. He made his way to the office of the aptly named Ethan Doom, the town's undertaker, and hammered on the door until the thin, pale-faced man in his fifties half-opened the door.

Dressed in a long, striped night shirt and holding a candle, Ethan relaxed somewhat when he saw it was the sheriff.

'Got another body for you, Ethan,' Ray said.

'Anyone I know?' asked Ethan.

'Will Lancaster. Went the same way as ol' Swampy.'

'Come in, Sheriff, while I get dressed and harness up,' Ethan said and opened the door wider.

Ten minutes later, Ethan was backing the wagon down the alley. Lancaster was a heavy man and, after rolling him on to a tarp, Ray and Ethan managed to lift him on to the wagon.

'You'll need a hand to get him off again,' Ray said.

'It's OK, Sheriff, I'll get Otis to give me a hand,' Ethan replied.

'OK, then ask Otis to come to the office, he's my new deputy,' Ray said, and waited for a response.

Ethan grunted, then said, 'He's a

good boy, you coulda done a lot worse. But he's young, he'll need to be taken care of.'

'I'll take good care of him,' Ray said as he left Ethan to carry on.

★　★　★

Chad and Burt Slim made steady progress riding north out of Bristow. They were heading to the Higgins' ranch with a foreclosure notice in their saddle bag — as well as their side irons and a Winchester each.

It was approaching midnight when they reined in on a small crest that overlooked the ranch house, which to the two men, looked more like a large shack.

There were no lights showing — they hadn't expected there to be any — these people worked in all the light the good Lord provided and slept when the sun went down.

Casually, Chad and Burt walked their mounts down the gentle slope.

They had been given their instructions by Curtis Waring, and they were quite specific: serve the foreclosure notice; put the fear of God in them and, whatever happens, there was to be no gun play — under any circumstances. He ordered the two men to return to the Silver Dollar when their job was finished, leaving their horses at the rear of the saloon. They would be taken care of later.

Waring had felt a slight twinge of guilt at the thought of evicting good people out of their home — and livelihood — but he quickly overcame that. After all, it was for the good of the town — and Curtis Waring.

The Higgins' place was plumb in line with the proposed railroad track. The land was flat and would make track-laying easy.

Chad and Burt remained in their saddles outside the shack. Chad took his Winchester out while Burt took out the foreclosure notice.

Using the Winchester's stock, Chad

hammered on the front door, sending slivers of wood falling onto the rickety porch.

Inside, Seth Higgins was awake in an instant. His wife, Martha sat up beside him.

'What on earth . . . ?' Martha said.

Seth got out of bed and lit a lantern which he handed to his wife. He then fetched his pistol, checked that it was loaded and told his wife to bring the lantern and stay behind him.

Cautiously, they made their way to the front door. 'Who's there?' Seth demanded.

'Bank business,' came the reply.

'Come back in the morning.'

'Nope. We got a notice here that has to be served,' Burt called out.

'What notice?'

'Foreclose, mister. You gotta get out of here in the next twenty-four hours.' Burt waited for a reply.

Shock, followed by anger and then defiance filled Seth's body as he yanked the door open and saw the two strangers. He levelled his pistol and, as Burt went to hand the foreclosure notice over, Chad pulled the trigger of his rifle.

Although only four feet from Seth, the slug passed through Seth's body, just catching him. Another inch and the bullet would have missed him entirely.

It twisted Seth round and as his finger squeezed his pistol's trigger, the bullet went harmlessly into the wooden floor.

But the slug that had pierced Seth's body hadn't finished yet. It caught Martha full in the stomach. It didn't kill her outright, but it sure would be a slow and painful death.

Martha was flung backwards, the lantern flew through the air as if in slow motion, before crashing to the floor and exploding in a ball of flame.

Seth tried to drag his nearly dead wife away from the flames, but his wound had sapped his strength.

Chad and Burt pulled their horses

back as the shack was quickly enveloped in flames.

'What the hell you do that for?' Burt snarled at his brother.

'He was raising his pistol. Self-defence, bro. Self-defence.'

From inside the shack the two men could hear the screams of children, trapped in their bedroom. The screams didn't last long as, in a whoosh of flame and sparks, the roof fell in.

Chad and Burt watched the conflagration, expressionless. Neither man spoke and, as an afterthought, Burt threw the foreclosure notice on the ground.

'Well, that's served,' he said to Chad.

'Leaves us in a bit of a quandary, bro.'

'How so?' Burt asked.

'Seems to me that banker fella, Waring, ain't gonna be too pleased 'bout how we handled this. Also, seems to me that sheriff is sniffing around, and he ain't too happy about us in general. He knows what we done, he jus' cain't prove nothin',' Chad replied.

'So what you thinkin'?' Burt said.

'Well, we bin paid $500 each up front, so we ain't short of dough. I reckon we hightail it outa this burg and jus' keep goin' north. What ya think?'

'Makes sense, I guess.'

'OK, let's move,' Chad said and pulled rein. 'We'll camp out in an hour or so. It'll be mornin', maybe, afore anyone sees this mess, by which time we'll be well clear.'

*　*　*

Waring was a worried man. It was after midnight and, although he'd sent Alfred round to the rear of the saloon to sort the horses out, there were no horses there!

'Just try once more, Alfred,' Waring said, his voice quivering slightly.

'Yes, sir, Mr Waring.' Alfred, eager to please as ever, dashed out of the office.

Five minutes later, Alfred was back.

'Sorry, sir, Mr Waring. Still no horses.'

'Thank you, Alfred, you may go home now. Not a word of this to anyone, understood?'

'Yes, sir.'

'You'll be well rewarded,' Waring added, trying to keep his voice calm.

'Thank you, sir, glad to be of service. Goodnight.' Alfred left the bank with a beaming smile on his face.

Smiling was the last thing Waring wanted to do. Something had gone wrong otherwise the Slim brothers would be back by now. They were either dead or . . . or what?

Or they'd run off with $1,000 of the bank's money! Money that, with the sale of the Higgins' place, would be paid back and no one would know. If they'd double-crossed him . . . Sweat now ran down Waring's face. If they'd done a runner, there was no way he could reimburse the bank at short notice.

Waring sat down, nervously drumming his fingers on the desk top and glancing towards the drinks cabinet.

He needed something to steady his nerves.

He sat and drank and eventually fell into a whiskey-induced sleep.

★ ★ ★

Sheriff Ray Cairney was woken from a deep sleep by banging on the office door.

He rolled out of the cell cot and stood a little unsteadily on his feet as he instinctively drew his pistol.

'Hold your horses, I'm comin',' Ray shouted.

'Sheriff, Sheriff, you better come on quick!'

Ray recognized the voice as that of old Wilbur — no one knew his surname, or even if he had one.

Ray pulled the two bolts and turned the key in the lock and opened the door. Wilbur almost fell through into the office in his excitement.

'What the hell, Wilbur?' Ray said,

grabbing the old man to stop him falling.

'You better come quick, Sheriff. I jus' been out to the Higgins' place and they's all dead!'

'What?' Ray was taken aback.

'Place was burned to the ground,' Wilbur said.

Ray was speechless. He'd known the family for a long time. 'They were good people,' Ray said, swallowing hard.

At that moment, Otis showed up, a huge grin on his face and his deputy's badge gleaming in the early morning sunshine.

'Mornin', Sheriff, Wilbur.'

The grin left Otis's face as he stared at the two men. 'Is something wrong, Sheriff?'

It was Wilbur who answered. 'The Higgins are all dead,' he said.

'I'm gonna have to throw you in at the deep end, Otis,' the sheriff said. 'I'll show you where the keys are for the cells and the gun rack. I'm sure you can get the stove on for coffee. I gotta go out to the ranch.'

'Sure thing, Sheriff. You can rely on me,' Otis said.

'You want me to come with you, Sheriff?' Wilbur asked.

'No. That won't be necessary, Wilbur. You did good in coming straight to me,' Ray answered.

After showing Otis the ropes, Ray unlocked the gun rack, took out a Winchester repeater and a box of bullets. He loaded the rifle, then made sure his Colt was loaded — with the chamber under the hammer empty, a safety precaution, he sure didn't want to shoot his own foot off!

'And Wilbur, not a word of this to anyone. That clear?' the sheriff said, giving Wilbur a steely glare.

'I'll be as silent as the grave,' Wilbur said, 'an' then some.'

Ray nodded and grabbed his saddlebags. 'I'll be back in a coupla hours, Otis. Shouldn't be any bother at this time of the day.'

'OK, Sheriff,' Otis said, feeling

slightly nervous.

With that, Ray left the office and headed for the livery. Five minutes later, he rode down Main Street, heading north.

'I'll be in the saloon if'n you need me, Otis,' Wilbur said.

'Thanks, Wilbur, but I think I can manage OK.'

Wilbur made his way to the saloon and Otis was left on his own.

Wilbur downed his first beer before he told the 'keep of his grisly discovery. There were already a dozen men in the saloon and word soon got round.

'That ain't the only thing that's happened,' the 'keep said. 'They found ol' Lancaster's body in a side alley, his throat cut from ear to ear!'

'Goddamn!' Wilbur said. 'What the hell's goin' on here?'

'An',' the 'keep continued, 'them two gunnies ain't around neither.'

'Who brung them two critters here in the first place?' Wilbur asked.

The saloon went quiet. Everyone

knew who brought the gunslingers into town.

'There's something weird goin' on in this town an' I for one don't like it.' Wilbur was the only man to speak. 'Fill me up, Charlie, I need beer!'

★　★　★

The ride out to the Higgins' ranch seemed like the loneliest and longest ride Ray had ever taken.

The small ranch, by American standards — 4,000 acres — was only two miles north of Bristow. Nevertheless, it took Ray nearly forty minutes to reach the same small crest where the Slim brothers had stopped.

Ray stared down the gentle slope at the still-smoking remains of the Higgins' place. The corral was untouched, and two jittery horses could be seen running from one side to the other. Ray was surprised they hadn't already broken out of the rickety corral. Maybe they were *too* scared, he thought.

Ray thought momentarily of rolling a cigarette, but he knew that was just delaying tactics. He didn't want to see what he knew he had to see down there in the charred remains of a once happy family home.

Reluctantly, he kneed his mount into a walk and descended the slope.

As he got nearer the ashy remains, the pungent smell of the smoke hit his nostrils, but there was something else, too. A sickly, cloying aroma that almost had him retching.

It was the smell of burning flesh.

Human flesh!

He reined in and brought his bandanna up to cover his mouth and nose and then dismounted, ground hitching his horse, who seemed as reluctant as the sheriff to go any closer.

Ray studied the soft earth surrounding the burned out shack. There were three sets of hoof prints. One, he knew, would be Wilbur's old donkey, and was easy to spot.

It was the other two sets he was interested in.

Careful not to disturb the hoof marks, Ray followed them to what was once a small porch.

Here they had stopped.

Neither rider had dismounted, so Ray assumed they had done their work from here. In his mind he played through a scenario. Higgins comes out, maybe holding a gun of some sort. It was a moonless night, so there had to be a lantern lit, carried by either Higgins or his wife. His wife, Ray decided.

Seeing Higgins was armed, one of the riders must have shot him, and, or, his wife. The lantern would have been dropped and that's how the fire had started.

But why? Robbery couldn't have been the motive, there wouldn't have been time to ransack the place. So what? What in hell did they kill them for?

Ray soon discovered the answer.

To his left he saw a slightly charred brown envelope.

'What the hell?' he said out loud.

Stooping, he picked the envelope up and tore it open.

'Hell an' damnation!' he uttered as he read the foreclosure notice. 'So that's what this is all about!'

He stuffed the paper into his saddle bags and followed the hoofprints. They headed north — away from Bristow.

Ray logged this information in his brain, then turned and walked back to the smoking ruin of the shack. He didn't want to do what he had to do next. He needed to confirm that the Higgins family was indeed, dead.

Keeping his bandanna tightly wrapped around his face, he reached into his saddle bags and brought out a pair of leather gloves.

Ray took a deep breath, and stepped gingerly into the burnt down place.

The first two bodies — if they could be called that — were just blackened remains, their mouths wide open in a silent scream, were lying at the front of the house.

By the side of one was the remains of an oil lamp. Slightly melted and the glass shattered.

Ray grabbed the legs of one of the bodies, and dragged it clear of the dark timber and onto the soft earth. Then he did the same with the second body, his stomach heaving as he did so.

He took half a dozen steps away from the bodies, tore off his bandanna and was violently sick. Taking deep breaths, Ray took control of himself and replaced the bandanna. Now he had to find the children.

He found them, huddled together in what had been their bedroom. To Ray, it seemed the boy had been protecting his sister. Although the lower half of their small bodies were burnt black, their faces were only slightly blistered.

Ray wept as he carefully lifted them and placed them by their parents.

Unrolling a tarp from his horse, he covered the bodies and, using the rocks that formed a border for a flower garden, he laid them round the edges. It should, he thought, protect them till Ethan got his buggy out here.

There was nothing more the sheriff could do out here and he made the decision to ride back to Bristow and confront Curtis Waring. He'd track down the Slim brothers later. He'd catch them — kill them if necessary — if it was the last thing he did.

5

The ride back to Bristow took just under forty minutes.

The sheriff's brain was racing. He knew who'd killed Swampy, Lancaster and now the entire Higgins family. But how to prove it?

He needed to break Curtis Waring and he meant to do it either within the law — or outside it. He had enough evidence in his saddle bags to arrest Waring for being an accessory to murder, at least for the Higgins' murders.

The sheriff reined in outside his office and went inside to check on Otis.

'Everything OK, Otis?' Ray asked.

'Sure is, Sheriff. Did the rounds. How was . . . er . . . is it true about the Higginses?'

'It is,' Ray replied. He unlocked the gun rack and put the Winchester back, but took out the scattergun.

'Trouble?' Otis asked.

'Just gonna pay our esteemed bank manager and town council leader a friendly visit,' Ray said, checking the scattergun's load.

'You need a scattergun?'

'Might not need to use it, but I need it nonetheless,' Ray said with a crooked grin. 'You hear shootin', you come a-runnin'. Head on over to Ethan's and tell him to get over to the Higgins' place. You better go with him cos he'll need a hand gettin' the wagon loaded. But be wary, it ain't a pretty sight.'

Otis sat at the desk, his mouth open with an unasked question. He stood and went to the window and watched as the sheriff strode purposefully to the bank.

Then he roused himself and dashed off to get Ethan Doom.

★　★　★

'That sure was a fine rabbit,' Chad said to Burt as he wiped his greasy lips on

71

the sleeve of his shirt.

The brothers had ridden a further thirty miles north of Bristow during the night, only stopping at sunrise to catch some food and maybe an hour's sleep. They were sure that no one would discover the burned down shack until daybreak and a posse, if they bothered to form one, would take a while to organize, so both men relaxed.

They had found the ideal campsite behind a huge boulder that had fallen many years ago and now rested by a swift running stream. The rabbit had been a stroke of good fortune.

Just as they were about to rein in, the rabbit darted across the trail. It was quick, but not quick enough. The right foreleg hoof of Chad's horse caught the rabbit full on the head. It died instantly.

'I'll take a quick nap now,' Chad said. 'Wake me in thirty minutes, then you take a nap while I keep watch. OK?'

'Sure. I figure they ain't nowhere near ready to come after us, but I guess it pays to be careful.'

Chad didn't need telling twice. Stretching out on the bare ground, he pulled his Stetson down over his eyes and was asleep almost instantly.

After both men had taken turns in sleeping, they splashed their faces with the cool water from the stream, drank their fill and made sure their canteens were full before mounting up again.

'Where shall we head, Chad?' Burt asked.

'Remember that rumour we heard down in Tucson?' Chad began.

'You mean about Jesse and Frank?'

'The very same. Seems they teamed up with the Youngers and, so the story went, are heading to the First National in Northfield.'

'Wouldn't mind getting a piece of that action,' Burt said.

'Me too, what say we mosey on up that way? If Jesse and Frank are there, all well and good. If'n they ain't, well, we'll head for Californy. Hear tell there's gold there for the takin'.'

'I'm with you, bro.'

Sheriff Cairney stormed into the bank, which was empty save for Alfred, who was brushing the floor near the front double doors.

'Waring in there?' the sheriff said through gritted teeth.

Alfred took one look at the scatter-gun and the blood drained from his face.

'Yes, sir, Mr Sheriff.'

'Open the door, Alfred,' Cairney said and waved the scattergun.

Alfred ran across the bank floor, nearly knocking over a small table, and unlocked the door that led to the cashiers' desks and Waring's office.

'Make yourself scarce, Alfred,' the sheriff said.

Alfred didn't need telling twice.

The office door was locked, but Ray lifted one boot and kicked it open. It flew back, banging on the wall next to the drinks cabinet, rattling the bottles inside.

Waring jumped out of his seat. 'What the devil — ' he began.

'Sit down, Waring.'

Waring slowly sank back into his leather chair, his face a bright red as sweat broke out on his forehead.

'What's the meaning of this, Sheriff? Bursting in here, damaging bank property — I'll have to report this!'

'You'll do it from inside one of my cells,' Ray said.

'You can't arrest me, I'm — ' Waring started to stay, but Ray cut him off.

'I can and I will.' Ray reached into his jacket pocket and pulled out the foreclosure notice. 'You sent the Slim boys to deliver this. They delivered it all right and killed the Higgins family!'

'What? I never — '

'You never what? Told them to kill?'

It was then that Ray noticed the map spread out on Waring's desk. He reached forward and turned the map to face him. It took him seconds to realize what was going on.

'So, the railroad's coming to Bristow!' Ray checked the railroad's proposed route and noticed the red crosses marked on the homes and ranches through which the track would pass through. Each plot of land had initials in black. CJ, WL, AL. Except now, the WL had been crossed out and either CJ or AL written in its place.

The missing initials were, of course, CW. Covering himself real well, Cairney thought.

'So you thought to buy cheap and sell dear, eh, Waring? You and Lowe and Jenkins? What did Swampy and Lancaster do that signed their death warrants? I can add fraud to the list now. You're finished, Waring. If I had my way, you'd hang just as surely as the Slim brothers will.'

Sheriff Cairney folded the map and stuffed it under his gun belt.

Panic set into Waring's face. He took out a kerchief and mopped his brow. 'Now look, Sheriff, surely we could come to some, er, arrangement. There's thousands at stake here.'

As he spoke, Waring teased open a drawer in his desk and felt around for the derringer he kept there. The exaggerated mopping was designed to distract the sheriff.

But it didn't.

Ray saw the movement and cocked the scattergun.

'Try it, Waring. They'll be scraping bits of you off'n the wall behind you for a week.'

Waring let the derringer fall back into the drawer and he closed it.

'You could make a fortune if you came in with us, Sheriff.'

'I'd rather sit in a nest of rattlesnakes. Get up, Waring and turn round.'

'You . . . you gonna . . . kill me?' Waring's voice shook in fear.

'I am the law, I don't break it,' Ray said as he took one of Waring's arms and slipped on the handcuffs he carried on his belt.

'Now walk,' the sheriff said, prodding Waring with the scattergun.

Waring stumbled forward, all the gusto, pomposity and bravado knocked out of him as he realized it was all over.

As the door to the sheriff's office opened and Waring stepped inside with the sheriff right behind him, Otis jumped to his feet, his mouth wide open in both surprise and shock.

'Lock him up, Otis. He'll be staying till the circuit judge arrives. I'm going to bring in Clint Jenkins and Ambrose Lowe, as well. They were all in it together.'

'All in what together, Sheriff?' Otis asked.

'I'll fill you in later, Otis. Allow no one, and I mean *no one* to come visit. You got that?'

'I got it, Sheriff. You can rely on me,' Otis said, puffing out his chest.

Otis took Waring to the cells and locked him in. He never, in all his life, thought his first day as a deputy would be like this and he couldn't help smiling.

Ray drafted two telegrams and handed them to Otis. 'I want this sent to every sheriff's office in every town north of here. And this one is for the federal marshal in Des Moines.'

Otis read the second telegram:

Evidence of corruption, fraud and murder involving the town council and two hired gunslingers stop. Curtis Waring, Clint Jenkins and Ambrose Lowe stop. The two gunslingers are Burt and Chad Slim stop. They are believed to be heading north stop. Signed Sheriff Ray Cairney, Bristow stop.

'Make sure you lock the office door,' Ray added. 'Sure thing, Sheriff.' Otis read the first telegram:

Slim brothers wanted for murder stop. Six dead here in Bristow stop. Armed and dangerous stop. Signed Sheriff Ray Cairney, Bristow stop.

Outside, Ray let out a long breath and rolled a cigarette. Inhaling deeply, Ray calmed down his nerves. He so wished Waring had made a play with that pistol he was holding. It would have given him great pleasure to spread Waring all over his office. The thought left Ray feeling slightly guilty. That was not the way the law operated.

He stubbed out his cigarette and mounted up, placing the scattergun in the scabbard by his left knee, then he set off to arrest the two ranchers, Lowe and Jenkins.

★　★　★

In the saloon, having a quiet drink before heading back to the ranch was Josh Kincaid, foreman of the Bar CJ, the ranch owned by Clint Jenkins.

He sat at his usual table, at the front of the saloon close by a window which afforded him a clear view of the street.

He watched with surprise as Sheriff Cairney marched a handcuffed Curtis

Waring along Main Street.

His immediate thought was this could be bad for his boss. Whatever Waring had been up to, as town council leader, he was pretty close to both Jenkins and Lowe, so was it possible they could be involved in some scheme?

It took Kincaid only seconds to decide to ride back and inform Jenkins of this development.

Casually, so as not to be noticed, he drained his beer glass, and said good day to Charlie.

'No rest for the wicked, huh?' Charlie said, grinning.

Kincaid didn't reply, merely tipped his bowler and headed for the batwings, relieved that no one else made any comment or looked his way.

Once outside, he mounted up and set off at a canter. The Bar CJ was just over four miles to the south of Bristow and he arrived within an hour.

Hitching his horse to the hitch rail outside the ranch house, he banged on the front door and waited impatiently for someone to answer it.

Miguel, Jenkins's cook and house-keeper and general dogsbody, slowly opened the door. A look of relief flooded his face as he recognized Kincaid.

'I gotta see the boss,' Kincaid said without preamble.

Miguel opened the door wider, saying, 'He's in study, Señor Kincaid.'

Kincaid pushed past the Mexican and walked straight into Jenkins's study.

'Josh! You ever heard of knocking?' Jenkins said irritably.

'Sorry, boss, but this could be important. I jus' seen Mr Waring, handcuffed, being marched off to the sheriff's office. Thought you should know.'

The colour visibly drained from Clint Jenkins's face.

'What, er, what was he arrested for?' Jenkins asked, his voice tremulous.

'That I don't know, boss,' Kincaid replied.

'I need you to ride back to town and

go into the bank.' Jenkins stood and opened a small safe set next to his desk. 'Here's $500. You keep a hundred for, er, your loyalty, bank the rest and see what information you can glean from the cashiers, or that errand boy Waring has working for him. One of them must know what the hell's goin' on.'

'Sure thing, boss, I'll get back as quick as I can.'

'You better send a man to Ambrose, let him know what's going on,' Clint added as an afterthought. 'You're a good man, Kincaid. I'll be here waiting.'

★   ★   ★

Sheriff Cairney had decided to tackle Ambrose Lowe first. His ranch was around three miles south east of Bristow. A 50,000 acre spread dealing mainly in cattle, but with a side-line of breeding horses. He had a good reputation as a breeder, and an even better one for his beef and was known as a fair man.

What, Ray pondered, had made him join in a scheme that had two men killed and a whole family murdered?

A phrase came into his mind, he'd no idea where he'd heard it, but it rang true: money is the root of all evil.

The sun had reached its zenith in the clear blue, cloudless sky and both man and beast were beginning to feel their energy being drained out of them.

Ray reined in and dismounted. He unhooked his canteen and took a few mouthfuls of the tepid water to slake his thirst. He then removed his Stetson and poured the rest of the water into it to let his mount drink. The river was only a half hour's ride away where he could refill the canteen and let his horse drink and wallow in the cool water.

Ray tensed. He strained his ears, turning his head from left to right and back again.

Distant hoof beats.

Scanning the horizon, he tried to pinpoint the rider but the sound was so far away it was difficult to get the direction.

Then he saw the dust cloud.

Whoever it was, was riding hell for leather. Ray figured he was running from something, or someone or maybe riding to somewhere. The only somewhere that Ray could think of was the Lazy AL, Ambrose Lowe's spread.

'Well, well,' Ray said to his horse. 'Seems to me word has got out.'

The horse whinnied in reply as if he understood every word.

Mounting up, Ray urged the animal forwards. 'Come on boy, we got some riding to do.'

Ray reached the river in record time and he leapt from the saddle to fill the canteen and allowed his mount a few minutes to drink his fill of the cool, clear water. Then he was off again.

* * *

Meanwhile, back at the Bar CJ, Clint Jenkins decided to take matters into his own hands. He rounded up some of his boys and told them of his plan to release Waring, who was being unjustly held in the sheriff's cells.

'It's important for the town,' Jenkins said. 'The sheriff has lost his mind, arresting our esteemed banker and chairman of the town council. He must be rescued. Any of you men who don't want to help might not have a future on the Bar CJ — or indeed in Bristow. So what do you say?' Jenkins finished speaking and looked at the half dozen men standing before him.

There was a pause before one man said, 'I'm in!' This was quickly followed by murmurs of assent from the rest of the group.

'Good, let's saddle up and do this!' Jenkins said. 'There'll be a little extra in your pay this week.'

This news was greeted with a cheer as the men ran to the corral to get their mounts. Within five minutes, the seven riders headed for Bristow.

Ray had lost sight of the distant rider, but was more certain now of his destination. There was no way Ray could either catch or beat the rider to the Lowe spread, so he just hoped he could get there and catch them by surprise.

He dug his heels into the horse's flanks. 'Come on boy, not far to go now.'

The unknown rider had already reached the Lowe ranch house and, spurred on by the promise of a bonus, he leapt from his horse and hammered on the front door.

It was Lowe himself who opened it, a derringer in his hand.

'What the hell do you want?' Lowe demanded.

'Mr Jenkins got word from town. The sheriff arrested Mr Waring and he's in jail.'

'What?' Lowe uncocked the derringer and put it back in his pocket

'Mr Jenkins thought you should

know, sir,' the man added.

'That damn sheriff!' Lowe grated. 'He's gotta go!'

Lowe handed the rider a ten dollar bill. 'You reckon the sheriff is on his way here?'

'I don't rightly know. I guess you'd know better than me.'

'There's another $20 in it if you stay here. I'll get some of the men ready — just in case.'

'Sure thing, I ain't got nothin' better to do, an' that darn sheriff is a mite too bossy for my likin'.'

'Good man. Corral your mount, there's feed and water in there,' Lowe said.

The rider tipped his Stetson and walked his horse across the courtyard to the corral and led him in.

Lowe sent out a piercing whistle that immediately had four men running from the bunk house.

'Get your weapons and spread out, we might have a mad sheriff on his way here an' he's likely to do anything, so be prepared. He's already arrested the town council's chairman on some trumped-up charge. There's $20 in it for each of you. Now, spread out and keep me covered if'n he does come here.'

The men grunted in unison.

'There's one of Jenkins's men here too, so don't mistake him for an enemy, OK?'

'Name's Ralph,' the rider spoke up. 'Where'd you want me, Mr Lowe?'

'Spread out from the barn, across the stables and down to the bunk house. That way we got crossfire, if we need it. But, whatever happens, don't shoot until I give the command. You all got that?'

Again, the men grunted.

'Right, let's get ready.' Lowe went back into the ranch house. He discarded the derringer and put on his gun-rig, checked the Colt was loaded, then placed a Winchester rifle by the door, where he could easily reach it, if need be.

When he was about a half mile from the ranch house, Ray reined in once more.

It occurred to him that, if Lowe had been warned, or informed, of Waring's arrest, there might well be a welcoming committee.

Ray scanned the terrain, looking for the best way to approach the ranch. If there was a trap set for him, it would be around the courtyard, the obvious way to reach the ranch house.

Ray decided to circle the ranch and approach the rear of the ranch house — they wouldn't be expecting that.

Slowly, Ray walked his horse in a semi-circle until he was at the rear of the ranch house. He dismounted and ground tethered his horse on a patch of lush grass. The horse whinnied in appreciation as Ray took the scattergun out of the scabbard and silently approached the house.

He was within ten feet when he saw movement at one of the windows. Ray stood stock still, waiting to see what would happen.

Nothing did.

The figure moved away from the window and Ray dashed to the side of the building and cautiously peered through that same window.

Inside he could see one half of the kitchen and a woman at the far end preparing vegetables. At the rear of the kitchen, he could see a door that led into the hallway. Ray took a deep breath and tried the rear door. It wasn't locked.

He slowly twisted the handle, hoping it didn't creak, until he was able to slide through the small gap. Walking almost on tiptoe, he crossed the floor to the hallway door and slid inside.

The hallway was empty, but Ray saw the Winchester leaning on the wall by the side of the front door.

There were two doors leading off the hallway. Ray decided to try the left hand side one first. He took out his Colt and silently cocked the hammer.

Opening the door quickly, he found it was a living room, crammed with ornaments and two large overstuffed leather armchairs, but no Ambrose Lowe.

Turning to the other door, he did exactly the same, opening the door with a rush.

Ambrose Lowe almost jumped out of his skin. He stood, meaning to go for his own gun, but Ray said, 'Go for that gun and you're a dead man!'

'How dare you — ' Lowe began.

'I am arresting you as an accessory to murder and attempted fraud, Lowe. You got anything to say, save it for the circuit judge.'

'That's preposterous,' Lowe said, sounding even more pompous than usual.

'I got all the proof I need,' the sheriff replied. 'Take off that gun belt. Now this is what we're gonna do. We're leaving by the front door, and my gun will be in your back all the way to the stable, so you better tell whoever is out there to hold their fire. Then we're gonna ride into town, where you can join Waring in jail.'

* * *

Clint Jenkins and his men rode in to Bristow and stopped outside the sheriff's office.

Jenkins dismounted and walked straight into the office.

Otis Culver leapt to his feet. 'Mr Jenkins, sir, what can I do for you?'

'You can release Curtis Waring for a start,' Jenkins grated.

'I don't think I can do that, sir,' Otis replied, wishing the sheriff was with him.

'I'm not askin', Jenkins said, 'I'm ordering you to release him!'

'Sheriff Cairney told me he's been arrested an' not to let anyone see him,' Otis protested.

'You either let him go or we'll bust him out,' Jenkins threatened, and took out his pistol.

'Whoa, there ain't no need for gunplay. I'm not takin' responsibility for your actions,' Otis said and tossed the keys to the cell to Jenkins.

Jenkins passed the keys to one of his men and turned to Otis. 'You'll do well here, son,' he said. 'The sheriff won't be around for much longer. As soon as we get a council meeting organized, he'll be given the sack. Which means we'll be lookin' for a new sheriff. You get my drift?'

Otis did, and he didn't like it one bit, but said nothing.

At that point, Waring came huffing and puffing from the cells, brushing the sleeves of his jacket as if he was bug infested.

'Thank God for some sanity around here,' he said.

'The situation has been made clear to the deputy here. I think we understand one another,' Jenkins said. 'We need to have a council meeting, the sooner the better.'

'Where's Ambrose?' Waring asked.

'I sent a man to him — to inform him of certain events and I'm sure he's taking, er, appropriate steps to remedy our predicament.' Jenkins nodded towards the deputy and Waring understood.

'Let's get to the bank,' Waring said. 'I need to take control.'

'First we gotta tie up young Otis here, don't want folks thinking he collaborated in freeing you,' Clint said.

'Good idea,' was all Waring said.

Having secured Otis to the sheriff's chair, the men headed for the bank.

★ ★ ★

The Slim brothers had reached the large town of Rochester, just south of Northfield, and here they decided to rest up awhile.

'Plenty of saloons for drinkin' and gamblin' and some fine looking fillies, I'll wager. Bound to be some green-horns we can take,' Burt said.

'Let's find a rooming house and get rid of this trail dust. A bath in a hot tub

an' a shave, then we hit the saloons.'
Chad smiled at his brother.

'Amen to that,' Burt said.

After asking around for a cheap
rooming house, they were given directions to Ma Boyle's, at the east end
of town, but not too far from the
centre.

Ma Boyle was a formidable character; a tall woman, maybe just on six
feet, and almost as wide as she was tall.

Dark hair tied up in a bun topped the
square-jawed woman with a ferocious
gaze.

'You got a room?' Burt asked.

'Sure, got a couple. How long you
stayin'?'

'A few days.'

'Two dollars a night, dinner included,
sort your own breakfast out. Bath's
extra and you sure both need one o'
them. No women, no boozin'. No high
jinks at all. I lock up at midnight an' I
don't open agen till dawn. Got that?'

'Yes, ma'am. One room, two beds,
and a bath each, if you please.' Chad

said, feeling a little intimidated by the huge woman.

'Makes no odds whether it's two to a room or you have a room each. Two dollars a person, bath's another dollar, in advance.' Ma Boyle folded her arms across her ample bosom.

'OK,' Burt said. 'Three nights, a room each, that's $12, and two more for the bath.' He peeled off $14 and handed it over.

Ma Boyle shoved the money down her dress top. Burt thought, that's a safer place than any bank!

'Top o' the stairs, first and second door on the right. I'll holler when the tub's ready.' She walked off without further comment.

★ ★ ★

Ray kept his Colt firmly pressed against Ambrose Lowe's spine as they opened the front door.

'You tell your men to hold their fire; you're one small click away from death,'

Ray said as he pushed Lowe forward.

'Hold your fire, men. I got a pistol to my back,' Lowe shouted.

'Tell them all to show themselves, hands held high, an' toss those weapons on the ground,' Ray demanded.

'You heard the man, come on out with your hands held high,' Lowe repeated.

One by one, the men came out from their hiding places. The clatter of rifles and pistols hitting the dirt was music to Ray's ears. All the men had their hands up.

'Now, one of you men saddle up Lowe's horse, and be quick about it,' Ray shouted.

One of the men ambled over to the stables.

'Bring the horse to the front door here and tether it. You walk back to the others,' Ray commanded. 'And no funny business. I'd as soon shoot him here as see him hang.'

'Now you an' me are gonna stand right here,' Ray said. He then put two fingers in his mouth and gave a loud whistle. A minute later, Ray's horse came walking round the side of the house and stopped at the front door.

Ray took out a pair of handcuffs. 'Hands together at the front. Now!' Ray pressed the gun in harder.

Slipping the handcuffs on, Ray relaxed slightly and pushed Lowe towards his disinterested horse. Reaching out with his left hand, Ray took down a short rope and waited for Lowe's horse to arrive.

Five minutes later, one of the men led Lowe's horse to the front of the ranch house.

'Now step back,' Ray ordered the man.

Then he slipped the rope between Lowe's handcuffed hands and looped it over the pommel of his horse. The other end he tied firmly to the reins of Lowe's horse.

'Right, mount up,' Ray ordered. 'An' remember, I got this here Colt just itchin' to see some action!'

Lowe clambered aboard his horse and at the same time, Ray mounted his own.

'Don't any of you boys get any ideas of following or trying to bushwhack. I got no argument with you and I sure don't wanna kill any of you.' Ray stared at each of the men in turn.

Pulling Lowe's horse closer to his own, he dug his heels into his mount and they set off for Bristow.

Ray felt most vulnerable at this point. His back was to the ranch hands so, twisting his head, he kept an eye on them, waiting to see if any of them made a move.

They got around fifty yards from the ranch hands when Ray saw a sudden movement. One of the men bent double and made a grab for his weapon.

As the man stood, his gun arm extended, Ray loosed off a shot and got lucky. From a moving mount and a gut-reaction shot, he saw the man fly back as the slug caught him full in the chest. He landed on his back some three feet from where he'd stood, raising a small cloud of dust.

'Goddamn! That wasn't even one of my men! That was Jenkins's hand,' Lowe said.

Ray ignored Lowe and dug his heels in, urging both horses into a canter. The sooner he was clear of this place the better.

★ ★ ★

The booming voice of Ma Boyle reverberated throughout the rooming house: 'Tubs are ready in the shack out back.'

'Jeez! You'd have to be stone deaf not to hear that,' Chad remarked.

'Or dead,' Burt added and both men laughed.

Grabbing fresh clothes, they headed for the tub shack. On the way, Ma Boyle handed each man a towel and a bar of rock hard soap.

'Hang the towels in the shack when you've done with them,' she ordered.

101

'Yes, ma'am,' the brothers uttered in unison, Chad giving Burt a wink and sly grin when Ma Boyle returned to the kitchen.

After they'd bathed, shaved and dressed in fresh duds, they were ready for whatever the night might bring. They were about to leave when Ma Boyle bellowed again.

'Supper's ready. Now!'

Almost sheepishly for hard cases like Chad and Burt, they turned tail and headed for the kitchen.

'Stew, dumplin's and bread,' Ma Boyle said. 'Coffee's on the stove, you can get that yourselves. Eat,' she commanded.

The brothers sat at the table as she placed two steaming bowls of stew with dumplings floating on top in front of them. It was then that the brothers realized how hungry they were.

There were two other people in the kitchen. A young boy, maybe eighteen or nineteen, and a dude dressed like a gambler with a pencil moustache. He wore a frock coat, white shirt with ruffles down the front, a gold coloured waistcoat and a bootlace tie. The brothers had seen his type many times.

Both men nodded a howdy as they ate. But no one spoke.

The young man got up to get a coffee and both Burt and Chad noticed his low-slung side iron and exchanged glances.

Finishing their meal, the brothers stood, shouted a thank you to Ma Boyle, put their Stetsons on and left the kitchen without acknowledging the kid or the gambler.

'Let's find a saloon,' Burt said, 'I got me a thirst.'

'Well, we don't have to look far,' Chad said. 'The Barrel House, let's try that.'

They crossed Main Street, dodging wagons and horses, and entered the saloon.

The air inside was thick with smoke and it took the two men a moment or two to get their breath but, as inveterate smokers, they soon got used to it.

They pushed their way to the long bar and ordered beer. The first one lasted ten seconds.

'Man, I needed that,' Burt said and ordered two more. They took their time over the second beer, taking stock of the saloon itself.

Ornately furnished, the saloon was split into two parts: the long bar which stretched down one side of the saloon was surrounded by tables and chairs and was obviously designed as a drinking area. The far side of the enormous open room, housed plusher chairs. Faro, roulette and poker tables filled the area and a giant lucky wheel stood in the corner.

The ceiling was festooned with lanterns and a large candle chandelier hung over the roulette table. At the back of the room, a piano player was thumping hell out of the keyboard which was set beside a small stage.

'Seems a decent enough place,' Chad said as he gazed around, 'and looks like they might have some dancin' girls here.' He broke out in a broad grin.

Above the din of the drinkers, the calls of the roulette croupier and the false laughter of the saloon girls, a shot rang out.

Suddenly the saloon went as quiet as the grave.

A poker table went flying as the recipient of the shot grabbed it as he fell backwards. Cards and chips and drinks went everywhere and, as Chad and Burt watched, two of the biggest men they had ever seen rushed to the stricken man and, wordlessly, dragged him away to the rear of the saloon.

The shooter was the dealer and the dead man, dressed in the usual manner of an itinerant gambler, obviously thought there was something untoward in the deals the saloon man was making.

But he'd been too slow. The dealer had been watching the man closely and recognized a disgruntled punter as, hand after hand, the man lost heavily.

The dealer, a man in his early thirties, or so Chad thought, was still holding the small derringer, spirals of smoke still wafting into the air.

A deputy appeared from nowhere and spoke to the dealer. Nodded, smiled, shook hands and left.

Chad and Burt exchanged glances.

'So that's how things operate round here,' Chad said.

'Better take care, bro. They bought the law here; that wasn't an ordinary handshake, neither,' Burt replied.

The two giants reappeared in the saloon and sat at a corner table. No one took any notice of them as the two hard cases kept their eyes peeled for any more trouble.

* * *

At every turn, Sheriff Cairney expected Lowe's men to wait in ambush. They could easily take the longer route to town and, at full gallop, could have got in front of himself and Lowe.

As the lights in Bristow started to appear in the distance, Ray began to relax slightly.

'You won't get away with this, Cairney,' Lowe grumbled.

'It's you who won't get away with it, Lowe. Six people, five innocent people and one of your so-called number have been killed. And for what? A quick buck?'

'It's more than a 'quick buck' as you call it. There's thousands at stake here and the town can only benefit in the long run.'

'You mean you, Jenkins and Waring will benefit. Foreclosing on ranches and homesteads, most of whom supply the town with food, will put the price of everything up. You know that. Not to mention the livelihoods you'll ruin. All you're interested in is yourself.'

'You're a fool. You could have been a rich man, but I tell you this, your days as sheriff of Bristow are coming to an end,' Lowe said.

'I can sleep at night, Lowe. Can you?'

Ray spat trail dust out of his mouth.

'I sleep just fine.'

Both men flinched as a rifle shot rang out and a plume of dust rose in the air as the slug hit the ground in front of the sheriff's horse.

'That's far enough, Cairney.' A voice shouted in a gruff tone, and at the same time eight riders appeared above a crest.

'Well, well,' Ray said. 'Your partners in crime have appeared.' Ray's hand slipped to the butt of his Colt.

'I wouldn't try that.' It was Waring who hollered, a crooked grin on his face. 'Told you you wouldn't keep me in jail,' he added.

'Enough chit-chat, turn Ambrose loose,' Clint Jenkins ordered, 'you're finished in Bristow.'

'Seems like I have no choice,' Ray said in a soft voice.

'None whatsoever,' Jenkins said.

'Throw down that Colt and unsheathe the rifle,' Waring ordered and Ray complied.

'Now what? You gonna kill me too?' Ray asked.

'No, we wouldn't kill an officer of the law — unless we had to!' Jenkins retorted. 'You just turn around and head north — and don't come back!'

'Now, release Mr Lowe,' Waring said.

Ray didn't move a muscle, but at a sign from Waring, the rannies they had brought with them drew their guns and cocked them.

'Thought you said you wouldn't kill an officer of the law?' Ray said.

'I said *we* wouldn't, but *they* might,' Waring answered, pointing at the men.

Grudgingly, Ray unlocked the handcuffs binding Lowe and released the halter from the man's horse.

'Now ride,' Waring commanded.

Ray wheeled his horse round and set off at a walk, no sense in tiring the animal, he thought.

Suddenly, he stopped. Turning, he called out, 'What happened to Otis?'

'Sheriff Otis is fine, don't worry

about him, we got him in our pockets,'
Waring replied.

'Hmm.' Ray didn't want to believe
that. He just hoped Otis was playing
possum until the federal marshal
arrived — if he ever did!

Ray walked his mount on.

6

The beers and whiskey chasers were going down well. Chad and Burt had found a table in the far corner, their gunslinging instincts always came to the fore when in a saloon. A corner table, their backs to a wall and as full a view of the surroundings as they could get.

They sat quietly for a while, checking the other tables, and keeping an eye on the poker table in particular. You could tell a lot about poker players just by watching their mannerisms, facial expressions, and any nervous movements.

Picking out the weak from the strong. Like a mountain lion chasing deer, they honed in on the weak.

'Seems like a nickel and dime game,' Chad remarked.

'Yeah, maybe it's too early for the real players to start.' Burt took out a Hunter pocket watch, flipped open the lid and peered at the dial.

'Eight thirty,' he announced. 'Ain't even dark yet.'

'Where in hell you get that watch?' Chad asked.

'Fella at the bar, didn't seem to mind,' Burt said and snapped the lid shut.

'Goddammit! We're tryin' to keep a low profile here, bro, afore we meet up with Jesse.'

'Hell, he won't miss it yet.'

But he was wrong.

There was a commotion at the bar and then a lot of pointing, all aimed at Burt and Chad.

'Goddamn! Now see what you done?' Chad said between gritted teeth.

Marching towards the brothers came three irate men who looked like they could take care of themselves.

Burt went to stand, but Chad stopped him. 'Play it cool, bro. Play it cool.'

'You stole my watch!' a large

barrel-chested man accused. 'An' I want it back. *Now!*'

'Hold your horses, mister. My brother found that there watch on the floor, we was gonna hand it over to the barkeep afore we left,' Chad said.

'That's a damn lie!' the big man thundered. 'That watch was in my vest pocket, where it always is.'

'You callin' me a liar, mister?'

'Cap fits, boy.'

'I ain't your 'boy.'' Chad was seething, barely unable to control his temper.

'I want my damn watch back!' the man reiterated.

Burt stood up slowly, reached into his vest pocket and pulled out a watch by the chain and dangled it towards the big man.

As the man went to grab it, Burt dropped it to the floor, then took a step forward and ground his heel into it.

The big man was purple with rage. Without thinking, he went for his gun.

He was fast, but not fast enough.

Burt drew his weapon and fired in

one smooth action, hitting the man plumb in the chest and sending him flying at least three feet backwards. In reflex, and already dead, the man pulled the trigger of his own gun as he was in mid-air, but all it hit was his own right foot.

The two men who had accompanied the dead man thought about drawing but, seeing the speed of Burt, they both raised their hands away from their sidearms.

'We don't want no trouble, mister,' one of them said.

'We don't neither,' Chad interjected.

At that point the two hard cases stepped into the fray. They didn't say anything, just lugged the body away in the same manner as the unlucky gambler.

Again the deputy entered, asked if it was self-defence, and three men said that Ernie, the dead man, had drawn first.

No one mentioned the watch.

Satisfied, the deputy left.

* ★ ★

Sheriff Ray Cairney had walked his horse for a further ten minutes before reining in and turning round. There was no way he was riding north unarmed and he hoped his weapons would be where he had been forced to throw them.

The posse, led by Waring, Lowe and Jenkins, had ridden straight back to Bristow, so eager were they to continue with their plans.

At a canter, Ray had reached the point where he had been halted and, sure enough, both rifle and hand gun were there in the tall grass by the side of the trail and there was no sign of the posse.

Dismounting, he picked up his guns, dusted them off, placed the rifle in the saddle scabbard and holstered his Colt.

Now he had to make a choice.

He mounted up, deep in thought.

There was little he could do in Bristow; the council had too many men with them and the likelihood was that he'd be killed trying to uphold the law. His only hope was that Otis had pretended to be with them and that the federal marshal would get there sooner rather than later. Once he saw the evidence that Ray had collected, he was sure to act on it and he doubted that Waring, Lowe and Jenkins would have the balls to murder a federal marshal.

Then there were the Slim brothers: the murdering scum had so far got off scot free. Ray was certain, by gut reaction, that the brothers had continued north.

Then it hit him: Rochester! That's where Ray would head for in their shoes. The town was big enough to get lost in, if that's what their intention was. He made up his mind; he'd take a gamble on Otis and the federal marshal and he'd track down the Slim brothers and make sure they got what they deserved.

Ray took off his sheriff's badge and

put it in his vest pocket. He was no longer constricted by the law.

★ ★ ★

Waring and his boys arrived back in the unsuspecting town of Bristow. There was now a sense of urgency to complete the six more foreclosures that he had set up. They had to be delivered pronto. Reining up outside the bank, the posse dismounted.

'You men have done well,' Waring said. 'Tell Charlie the drinks are on the house; the town council will settle up. Tomorrow morning I'll have another job for you and don't worry, you'll be well rewarded.'

The six hands were more interested in the free drinks, but the promise of more dough was a bonus.

Waring waited until the men had entered the saloon before ushering Jenkins and Lowe into the bank.

Alfred leapt to his feet. 'Mr Waring, sir. Good to see you, er, free,' he said, unsure of what had gone on.

'Coffee, Alfred and plenty of it,' Waring said. 'Then I'd like a quiet word with you.'

'Coming right up, sir,' Alfred said, uncertain of what a 'quiet word' meant.

Waring ushered his two partners into his office, opened the drinks cabinet and took out a bottle of single malt whisky, specially ordered from Boston.

'Gentlemen, the finest Scottish whisky there is,' and poured three shot glasses with the amber liquid.

Handing each man a glass he said, 'Gentlemen, to success,' and raised his glass.

The three men downed their whisky in one gulp and Waring replenished their empty glasses.

'Now, we have no time to lose. I have already drawn up the foreclosure notices on the remaining ranches and homesteads we need to, er, acquire.' He smiled broadly. 'Tomorrow morning at sunrise we'll deliver them and in two days' time, we'll have the entire route the railroad company is planning to purchase.

'We will, of course, need more men now that those Slim boys have high-tailed it. But I'm sure that, between you, we can rustle them up.'

There was a knock at the door. 'Come in, Alfred,' Waring shouted.

A sheepish Alfred entered, carrying a tray with three cups and saucers and a pot of steaming coffee.

'Ah, Alfred, good man,' Waring said genially.

Alfred poured the coffee, a hint of a smile on his face. He was about to leave when Waring said, 'Take a seat, Alfred, there's something I need to discuss with you.'

Apprehension now replaced the smile on Alfred's face as he sat down, bolt upright, hands on knees.

'You are, I believe, good friends with Otis, or I should say, *Sheriff* Otis.'

'Sheriff?' Alfred almost stuttered.

'Yes, Mr Cairney is no longer a representative of the law in Bristow,'

Waring stated. 'Now, I need to find out if Cairney left anything with Otis before he rode out. Do you think you could maybe have a chat with Otis? Friendly like, see what you can find out.'

Alfred was quiet for a few moments, his mind racing. What were they after? Why did they want him to spy on his friend?

'There will shortly be a new position opening up in the bank for a junior teller and I'm sure that, if you play your cards right, that position could easily be filled by you. Of course, it would mean more money,' Waring added.

'Well, er, of course, Mr Waring. I could try,' Alfred said falteringly, his brain whirling at the thought that he was now being asked to spy *and* being bribed. It must be something mighty important to Mr Waring, he thought.

'Good man, Alfred, I knew I could rely on you,' Waring said magnanimously.

Without being told, Alfred knew the

interview was over and he stood and made his exit.

* * *

Alfred was in turmoil. Stuck between his friendship with Otis (the two had grown up together and been the best of friends) and his loyalty to the bank, and in particular, Curtis Waring.

He left the bank and walked down the street, heading for the sheriff's office, his intention to speak with Sheriff Otis Culver. Alfred smiled as he thought, *Sheriff Otis Culver*.

In the hundred yards or so that he'd walked, Alfred made his mind up to not spy on his friend, but tell him what he'd been asked to do.

Reaching the office, he knocked on the door and entered.

Otis was sitting at his desk, leafing through Wanted posters. He looked up to see his old friend.

'Alfred, good to see you. I guess you know what's been going on. The town council sacked Sheriff Cairney and gave me the job, but I sure don't like it.' Otis stood and shook hands with Alfred.

'What brings you down here, anyway?' Otis asked.

Falteringly, Alfred told Otis about the conversation he'd had with Waring, leaving nothing out.

'But I couldn't bring myself to spy on you, Otis,' Alfred finished.

'I appreciate that, Alfred. I'll tell you nothing, that way you won't be lying to Mr Waring. But I'll tell you this much, Sheriff Cairney uncovered some pretty damning evidence that implicates your Mr Waring and no doubt, the rest of the town council.'

'Don't say any more,' Alfred said.

'OK, but I wanted you to know that something's going down here and hopefully, a federal marshal will be arriving soon.'

Alfred had gone quite pale.

'Coffee?' Otis asked.

Alfred nodded. In his mind he could see his prospects at the bank rapidly diminishing and all through no fault of his own.

Otis handed Alfred a mug of coffee and the two men sat in silence for a while, until Otis said, 'How'd you feel about informing me of anything you hear at the bank, Alfred?'

'Reckon I could live with that, old buddy.' Alfred smiled.

Both men drained their coffee and as Alfred stood to leave, Otis said, 'Just be careful out there, OK?'

They shook hands and Alfred left to go back to the bank, dreading further interrogation from Waring, but at least he was prepared for it.

★ ★ ★

Ray Cairney had been riding at a steady canter for nearly four hours. It was late afternoon and the heat was beginning to subside as he saw a wisp of smoke in the distance.

With no food and little water, Ray hoped it was a friendly homestead.

Maybe get some grub and, with a bit of luck, somewhere to sleep.

As he drew closer, Ray decided to put his sheriff's badge back on his vest. He didn't want anyone to think he was a drifter, a no-good.

He caught sight of a woman, crossing from the barn, carrying what looked like a bundle of washing.

At almost the same time, the woman saw the rider. Immediately, she dropped the bundle and ran to the house, emerging a few seconds later with a rifle.

'I mean you no harm, ma'am,' Ray said and raised both hands high in the air. 'I'm Sheriff Ray Cairney from Bristow and on the trail of two bloody killers.'

'If you're a sheriff, where's your badge?' the woman asked.

Ray lowered one hand and opened his dust coat to reveal the badge of office.

'Ride in, but slow,' the woman commanded and Ray did as he was told. 'Now throw down that side iron.'

'I'd rather not, ma'am. Takes a heap o' time to clean it up. But I will hand it to you, butt first.' Ray tried a half-smile.

Ray walked his mount right up to the woman and began to draw his Colt.

'Left hand!' she ordered, and Ray handed her the Colt with his left hand.

'Now the rifle, again, left hand.'

He handed over the rifle and this time gave a full smile.

'I guess you can water your horse,' the woman said. 'Trough over by the barn.' She pointed.

'Thank you kindly, ma'am. I was wonderin' if you had any spare vitals, I'll gladly pay.'

'I can rustle up some. I got some stew that's about ready, you're welcome to have some.'

'That would be most welcome, ma'am,' Ray said.

'And stop calling me ma'am. My name's Sue.'

'Sue it is then; please call me Ray.'

Ray walked his horse to the trough,

let it drink for a while then tethered it to a corral post.

'Nice place you got here,' Ray said, stripping off his range coat and shaking the trail dust from it.

'Thank you. It's hard work, but I enjoy it.'

'If'n you don't mind me askin', there no menfolk here?'

Sue bristled slightly before answering.

'My husband was killed almost two years ago,' she replied.

'Sorry to hear that, ma' — Sue. Didn't mean to pry.'

She didn't elaborate. 'You can camp out in the barn, there's plenty of hay in there. It'll be dark in an hour,' Sue said, in what to Ray sounded like a nervous voice.

'I 'preciate that. I'll be outta your hair come sunup.'

'I'll sort some provisions for you. There isn't much, but I'll do what I can.'

Ray took out his billfold.

'I don't want your money,' Sue said, 'but if you have any spare .45s, that would be more useful to me.'

'Sure have, I'll get a box from my saddle bag now.'

'Thank you,' Sue said, a little embarrassed at being so forthright. 'Maybe your horse could do with some oats — there's some in the barn, help yourself. I'll serve up some stew, before you go.'

'Thank you, Sue. Kind of you. An' that was a mighty fine stew, I'm fit to bustin',' Ray said with a silly grin on his face after he'd eaten.

While Sue tidied away the dishes and put the rest of the stew back on the stove, Ray took a good long look at her.

Her shoulder-length brown hair hung loosely about her face. A face that would hearten any man. Ruby red lips that seemed in a permanent pout that sent a shiver down his spine. Her large green eyes sparkled as she washed the dishes and her figure-hugging jeans and shirt didn't deny her femininity.

Ray felt as though he was in a daydream as he gazed at her, and when she turned suddenly to ask if he wanted coffee, he felt himself blush, as if he'd been caught spying on her.

'Er, sure, yes please,' he managed to say, his voice thick.

Sue noticed his embarrassment and he caught sight of a smile as she turned back to the stove.

'I'll get those slugs,' Ray said and left the house and walked across to the barn. His horse whinnied as he approached. 'Don't worry, boy, getting you some food now.'

He filled his Stetson with oats and walked back to the horse, placed his hat on the ground and patted the animal, then opened his saddle bag and took out a box of .45s. There were ten boxes in there, 20 slugs to a box, he worked out, 200 slugs in all, more than enough. He took out a second box and smiled.

The sun was almost setting, the red glow to the west sinking fast. The slight breeze felt cool and refreshing as it caressed his face and Ray felt unexpectedly happy.

He walked back to the house, noting how beautiful the scenery was, something he rarely did, and he smiled — broadly.

He handed over the bullets, their fingers touching as he did so, and Ray felt what he could only describe as an electric shock. The only time he'd ever felt that before was when a bolt of lightning hit a tree nearby and he got a mild shock.

He saw Sue blush slightly, only enhancing her beauty, and then he knew she had felt it too.

Awkwardly, he said goodnight.

'I'll show you where you can put your horse, and where you can sleep,' Sue said. Equally awkwardly.

* * *

'That was a fine damn watch you jus' destroyed,' Chad said. 'We coulda sold that for a few dollars.'

129

'Weren't his watch, was my old one that ain't worked in months, ever since we was caught up in that sandstorm.' Burt grinned at Chad.

'Son of a gun, you dog,' Chad said, laughing.

'Don't matter which way, I guess we better cut an' run. Maybe find another saloon afore we go to bed,' Burt said. 'Lotta folks staring at us now.'

'Good thinking. We'll wander down a ways and see what gives.' Chad was already heading for the door. Burt started to follow.

'Hold up a while, boys,' a genial voice asked. 'Let me buy you a drink. That Ernie was always mouthin' off. Too big fer his breeches.

'Name's Earl, Jed Earl, gotta proposition that would suit two fine men who know how to handle a gun,' Earl went on.

'An' what sorta proposition would that be?' Chad asked.

'The kind that pays $500 for a few minutes' work,' Earl replied, guiding them to his table, where there was already a full bottle of bourbon and three glasses.

'Take a seat and help yourselves,' Earl said.

Chad poured three fingers into each of the shot glasses and downed his in one go. Earl sipped at his and Burt left his glass on the table.

'So, what do we have to do for $500?' Burt asked.

'Kill a man,' Earl replied, filling his and Chad's glass again.

'Any partic'lar reason?' Chad asked.

'Nothing that need concern you. Let's just say he has something I want and the only way I can get it is for him to be dead.' Earl looked at each man in turn.

Burt picked up his drink and downed it in one, refilling it again.

'I got no problem with that,' Burt said. 'Providing we get the money up front.'

'Two-fifty as a down payment and another two fifty when the job is done.

That fair enough?' Earl again looked from one man to the other.

'Let's see the colour of your money,' Chad said.

Furtively, looking all around him, Earl placed his hand inside his coat pocket. Instinctively, both Chad and Burt placed their hands on their pistols.

'Whoa! No need for that,' Earl said, 'just getting the money out.'

Keeping his fist bunched, Earl placed a roll of notes on the table, but kept his hand on it. 'Too many prying eyes,' he said, winking.

Chad leaned forward and covered Earl's hand, Earl removed his hand, and Chad grabbed the money. Under the table, he flicked through the notes.

'Seems to be all here,' he said to Burt. 'OK, when, where and who?'

'The 'when' is as soon as possible. The 'where' is up to you. The 'who' is over at the bar right now. White Stetson, green shirt.'

Chad and Burt scanned the men at the bar until they saw their quarry.

'He don't look up to much,' Burt commented.

'Just a kid, by the looks,' Chad added.

'Be that as it may, he's the man I want dead, savvy?' Earl said.

Burt stood. 'Watch my back, bro,' he said to Chad.

Calmly, he walked to the bar and stood beside the man in the green shirt. He took out a five dollar bill and dropped it on the floor.

'Hey, mister, looks like you dropped some money there.' Burt pointed to the note.

As the man stooped to retrieve the bill, Burt drew his knife and slit the man's throat in one easy motion. He even had time to wipe the blade clean on the man's bandanna.

Green shirt fell, face down, and the men around him laughed. 'Too much to drink, eh, Jed,' one said mockingly. Burt had gone back to his table before anyone saw the rapidly spreading pool of blood.

'Jeez!' His drinking buddies turned the body over and saw the deep, red, slash across the man's throat.

'Quick, someone get the doc! He ain't dead yet!'

Blood gurgled from the man's throat as he fought, in vain, to breathe and stay alive. After three minutes, the gurgling stopped and the blood flow began to ebb and Green shirt breathed his last.

'That's $250 you owe us,' Burt said nonchalantly, filling his glass with bourbon as if nothing had happened.

Earl sat open-mouthed at the audacity of the killing; he couldn't quite get his head round it.

'Er, yeah, sure.' Earl fumbled in his coat pocket and brought out the money, again keeping it in his hand palm down, and as Burt covered his hand, Earl withdrew his and Burt checked the money under the table.

'Seems our business here is done,' Chad said. He drained his glass and he and his brother left the saloon.

Earl sat speechless.

But now Earl would offer his condolences to the beautiful widow of Jed.

He smiled.

7

Ray woke from a troubled sleep. His brain was buzzing, tossing between what he knew was his duty in bringing the Slim brothers to justice and the feelings that were growing for Sue. He kept seeing her face in his dreams as it transmogrified into the Slim boys.

That woke him up.

Standing, he stretched his weary frame and walked to the water trough, shirtless. He splashed cold water over his face and then over his upper torso. That *really* woke him up.

Sue was standing in the doorway of the house, watching him wash. She noticed his taut, muscular body and shivered, dismissing the thoughts that filled her head.

When Ray had finished, she called out to him, 'Breakfast is ready.'

Ray, caught by surprise, almost

jumped, feeling slightly embarrassed at his state of undress.

'Be right there, ma' — Sue,' he stuttered, the awkwardness returning.

Quickly throwing on his shirt, he fumbled with the buttons in his haste to get it on. 'Pull yourself together,' he muttered to himself and took several long, deep breaths.

Entering the house, the aroma of bacon with a background of freshly brewed coffee filled his nostrils and his mouth watered.

'Morning, Sue,' he said.

'Morning, Ray,' she answered.

There was a thick atmosphere between them, each having thoughts they couldn't voice — at least, not yet.

'Take a seat, eggs are ready,' Sue said, merely to make conversation.

They ate in silence, each casting furtive glances at the other and averting their eyes when eye contact was made.

When he'd finished eating, and drained the last of the coffee, Ray stood. 'Thank you, Sue, that was a great breakfast.'

'You're welcome,' she replied. 'I've packed a few things for your journey in a gunny sack. It's there on the sideboard.'

'Thank you again, I'll return the sack.'

'I hope so.' Sue blushed sweetly.

Ray smiled, showing white, even teeth. 'I best be going, there's a storm brewing.'

'Take care and make sure you bring that sack back.' Sue quickly pecked him on the cheek.

To Ray, it felt like a branding iron — without the pain. His head was swimming in delight as he saddled up. Mounting, Sue ran over holding the sack.

'You forgot this,' she said, smiling.

'Be seeing you — soon, I hope,' Ray said and tipped his Stetson.

'I hope so, too,' she replied demurely.

★ ★ ★

Ray set his horse to a steady canter, heading north. The sun's rays were warm on his back and his heart wanted to stay with Sue, but he knew what he had to do.

He could be wrong, he thought. Maybe the Slim brothers didn't head for Rochester and this would turn out to be a wild goose chase. He only hoped that Otis had hidden the foreclosure notice and the map and that a federal marshal would visit Bristow.

And then there was Sue.

Ray's head was spinning. He knew he had to pull himself together and concentrate on the job in hand. There was no way you could track down two vicious killers with your head in the clouds.

He had no tracks to follow, just his own gut reaction. Putting himself in the same position as the Slim brothers, he was following what *he* would have done, and he headed for Rochester.

By mid-afternoon, the sheriff was just

five miles south of Rochester. The weather had begun to change as the day wore on, summer was over and fall was beginning to take over. In this part of the country the change of season was often dramatic, sunshine one day, snow the next. There was a chill in the air and clouds scudded across the sky. He knew it wouldn't be long before the snows came, laying a blanket of white across the landscape.

When he was barely two miles south of Rochester, Ray could smell the town before he could see it. The head wind carried with it the smells of smoke, beer and tobacco fumes and, after the crystal clear air of the prairie, civilization? Ray pondered.

He reined in and dismounted and, after watering his horse, rolled a cigarette and inhaled deeply. Was he on a fool's errand? Only time would tell.

He finished his cigarette and mounted up. His stomach rumbled, but he figured on keeping his rations and eating in Rochester as he didn't know what he'd do if there was no trace of the killers. He rode on.

* * *

'Best we high-tail it outa here, bro,' Chad said. 'The law might be bought in this town but we're strangers, the sheriff might want to make an example of us to please his bosses. What do you think?'

'Yeah, I agree,' Burt replied. 'Tired o' this place anyways. We got a good stake, let's ride.'

* * *

After the quiet of the prairie, the hustle and bustle of a prosperous town sounded like thunder in Ray's ears.

The weather had taken a turn; thick black clouds obscured the sun, bringing a premature twilight. Already stores and offices were showing lantern light and as he rode down Main Street, a man was busy lighting the street lanterns, their soft yellow glow casting eerie shadows.

His first port of call was at the livery stables, making sure his horse was watered and fed and given a good brush down to get rid of the trail dust, and now it was his turn.

Following his nose, he found a small café that had a bill of fare in the window. Prices looked reasonable and he went in.

There were eight tables, three unoccupied, and Ray chose one by the front window where he had a good view of Main Street.

'What'll it be, stranger?' A young waitress with long red hair and the brightest blue eyes he'd ever seen and a smile as broad as the Mississippi had approached him.

'Gotta be steak, rare, biscuits and tatters,' Ray replied.

'Coffee?'

'Yes, please, I could drink a bucketful,' Ray said smiling.

'Coming right up,' the waitress said and walked back to the kitchen.

* * *

Out on Main Street, the Slim brothers walked their horses, trying to be as inconspicuous as possible. They were leaving town. They'd checked out of their rooms, the clerk apologizing because he wasn't allowed to give refunds. Strangely, the sight of Burt's frontiersman right under his nose gave him a sudden change of heart.

Chad suddenly stopped. 'Burt, café window!'

'Goddamn! Ain't that the sheriff of Bristow?'

'Sure is. Let's keep riding and we'll figure what to do about it,' Chad said and heeled his horse into a walk.

* * *

Ray finished his meal and drained the last of his coffee as the waitress reappeared. 'We got some homemade apple pie,' she said, again the beaming smile.

143

'Miss, that was the best steak I had in a long time and I'm full to the rafters, but thank you anyways,' Ray said, placing $5 on the table.

'That's a dollar too much,' the waitress said.

'The extra dollar is for your smile.' Ray surprised himself that he'd said it out loud.

The waitress blushed a deep red, but the smile was still there.

'Thank you kindly,' she said as she picked up the money. She walked back towards the kitchen, giving Ray a glance over her shoulder as she went.

Ray stood, put his Stetson on and said, 'Bye' as he left the café. Now he needed a drink. The Barrel House was opposite, so he decided to head on in there; they might even have a room for the night if he was lucky.

The saloon was packed and raucous; the piano was going full tilt and the sounds of laughter and general conversation sounded like thunder after the silence out on the prairie.

Ray fought his way to the bar top and ordered a beer. 'You got a room for the night?' he asked the barkeep.

'Sure, single or double? We got some fine young fillies working here,' the barkeep said with a wink.

'Just a single,' Ray replied.

'Suit yourself,' the barkeep said as he placed a frothy glass of beer on the counter. 'Room's $4, beer's 50 cents.'

Ray handed over a ten, but held on to it.

'I'm looking for two fellas who might have come this way. You seen two strangers recently?'

'Mister, I see strangers every day, in fact, I'm talkin' to one now!'

'I'm Sheriff Ray Cairney of Bristow, and these two fellas're brothers and vicious killers, so I need to know if'n you seen any strangers that might fit. Both around six feet tall with long hair, clean shaven last I saw 'em. They're vicious killers,' Ray reiterated, urging the man to think.

'I see'd 'em,' a voice behind Ray piped up.

Ray spun round. 'See'd, I mean, seen what?'

'Them two fellas.'

'How do you know?'

'They shot Ernie over yonder when he went to get his pocket watch back, an' I see'd one of 'em slit the throat of another man, right where you be standing, mister. No one else see'd that, but I did.'

'You know where they're stayin?' Ray asked.

'Nope. But if I were a bettin' man, I'd start at Ma Boyle's rooming house,' the old man replied.

'Thanks, mister. 'Keep, get this man a drink.'

Ray finished his beer in one gulp and left the saloon.

★　★　★

At the north edge of town, the Slim brothers reined in and set to parley.

146

'Sure thing the sheriff is alookin' fer us,' Burt said. 'We gotta do somethin' 'bout that.'

Chad agreed. 'Chances are he'll carry on headin' north so I figure we set up camp just off the main trail and bushwhack the sonuvver. What do you think?'

'Sounds like a plan,' Burt agreed.

They spurred on, intent on finding a good spot to camp. Some three miles north of Rochester, they found the ideal spot not far from a river. An outcrop that provided shelter from the wind and would allow them to build a small fire that wouldn't be seen from the trail.

'I'll gather some kindlin' and get the fire goin',' Chad said. 'We'll take turns in keepin' watch, there's a good view from the top of the rocks, there.'

He pointed to a smooth, flat rock about ten feet above them.

'Doubt he'll come tonight. But sure as eggs is eggs, he'll be ridin' out at sunrise,' Chad continued as he gathered kindling and began to arrange it Indian style — there would be little or no smoke to give their position away.

Burt took the Winchester out of its scabbard and loaded it, checked his Colt, grabbed his bedroll and clambered up the rock to settle himself comfortably.

'See for miles up here, Chad,' he said in an almost boyish voice. 'Sure is purty!'

* * *

Ma Boyle wasn't exactly the friendliest of people and didn't take too kindly to being disturbed during what she called her quiet time.

Ray was insistent, plying her with questions and grudgingly, she answered in monosyllables, with a 'yep' or a 'nope'.

'Them two in their room?' he asked.

'Nope.'

'You seen 'em this evening?'

148

'Nope.'

'You checked their rooms?'

'Yup.'

'Their gear there?'

'Nope.'

'Reckon they've left?'

'Yup.'

'You see which way they were headed?'

'Nope.'

'They give a name?'

'Nope.'

'Sure has been nice chattin' with you, ma'am,' Ray said sarcastically and tipped his hat. The sarcasm was lost on Ma Boyle.

Ray quickly made his mind up on the next course of action. His hunch had been right and he was close to the Slim brothers. He made his way back to the livery and saddled up, paid for some extra oats and barley and filled his canteen.

He was ready to ride.

★　★　★

Federal Marshal Tom Brown had received a telegram from the sheriff of Bristow and decided to ride on up there and see what the trouble was.

It was a six hour ride at a steady canter and Brown arrived in Bristow just as the sun began to sink in the west, casting long tendrils of orange and creating a vast array of long shadows. He rode straight to the sheriff's office and walked in.

Otis jumped to his feet as he saw the silver badge pinned to Brown's vest.

'Sheriff around?' Brown asked without preamble.

'I'm acting sheriff,' Otis replied. 'Sheriff Cairney has gone after two killers. He left yesterday.'

'You got somethin' to show me?'

'Sure have, Marshal.' Otis walked to a war bag hanging by the office door and took it down.

The marshal sat at the desk and removed the two documents, and checked the foreclosure notice first.

'This looks perfectly legal,' he said.

'It was found outside the home of the Higgins family. Higgins, his wife and two children were burned to death. Sheriff Cairney is after the killers who left the note on behalf of the bank.' Otis took a deep breath.

'And the map?'

'As you can see, the Higgins' place has been wiped clean and a green tick added. The rest, which seem in a straight line, have red crosses,' Otis informed the marshal.

'And the initials? I see WL has been crossed out,' the marshal said.

'The town council. There are four members. Will Lancaster is dead; CJ is Clint Jenkins; AL is Ambrose Lowe.'

'You said there were four,' the marshal looked up at Otis.

'The fourth man is the banker, Curtis Waring,' Otis told him.

'Now why ain't *his* initials on this map? He's the man who forecloses. Maybe that's why. What could be so important about these properties?'

Otis said nothing.

'I think I'll pay this Mr Waring a visit,' Brown said. 'But first, get that coffee on.'

★   ★   ★

The arrival of a federal marshal hadn't gone unnoticed.

As was his custom, Waring had locked the bank and went to sit on a rocker. He took out a large cigar and puffed away contentedly. His scheme was going to plan and, with Cairney out of the way, nothing could stop him now.

It was unfortunate, to say the least, that the Higgins family had been killed; Lancaster was no great loss. Maybe he'd foreclose the saloon as well? That would make a nice little sideline. He'd keep that thought to himself.

Pretty soon, Bristow would be his. He'd be lord of the manor and as the town prospered, so Curtis Waring would be the most powerful man in town.

He sat, waiting patiently for Jenkins

152

and Lowe to arrive. They, and their men, would serve the remaining foreclosure notices at first light, then he could sit back and wait for the cash to come rolling in.

He smiled.

At first, the stranger walking a huge black stallion down Main Street only raised a passing curiosity in Waring. The town was used to the odd stranger arriving.

But his attention intensified when he caught a brief glimpse of something shiny on the man's vest as the fading sunlight illuminated it.

A badge!

Waring tensed. He knew it couldn't be another sheriff, they only had jurisdiction within their own town limits. That left one alternative.

A federal marshal!

'Damn it all to hell!' Waring said under his breath. 'What in tarnation is a fed doing here?'

He hurried down to the Silver Dollar. Surely his men would arrive soon and as he thought that, he heard hoofs, plenty of them, riding down Main Street.

'Thank God!' Waring said out loud. He saw Jenkins and Lowe leading around ten men towards the Silver Dollar.

'Inside. Quick!' Waring called out.

The look of alarm on Waring's face precluded the two men from asking any questions. They dismounted and followed Waring.

'You men get a beer, on the house,' Waring called back over his shoulder.

Once inside, Waring led the two men into Lancaster's old office.

'A federal marshal has just arrived in town,' Waring blurted out. 'I've just seen him ride past the bank.'

'What the hell — ' Lowe began.

'You reckon Otis called him in?' Jenkins asked.

'I doubt it,' Waring said, his mood pensive. 'It could only be Cairney! He must have called him in. Otis hasn't the wits — yet.'

'What're we gonna do?' Lowe asked. 'We can't possibly go ahead now.'

'We've come too far to stop now,' Waring said. 'We'll have to take care of the marshal.'

'You mean kill him? Kill a federal marshal? We'll have the whole weight of the law down here in no time.' Lowe shook his head.

'Not if we kill him here and dispose of the body out on the prairie. Make it look like he was bushwhacked,' Waring replied.

'We've got enough men, and, with a special bonus, I'm sure they can carry out the job. Remember, there's a lot at stake here. Tomorrow, I plan to start transferring the title deeds of the properties into your names, ready to sell to the railroad company. We can't stop now!' Waring watched the faces of the two men as they considered what other options they had.

There were no other options.

'I'll call my foreman in,' Lowe said and left the office.

★ ★ ★

Sheriff Cairney was riding slightly to the right of the main trail that led directly to Northfield, Minnesota.

His trained eye scoured the trail ahead, seeking out any fresh tracks, but his task was almost impossible as the trail was well-used, but he was ever vigilant.

Ray felt the slug just before he heard it. It whistled over his right shoulder, leaving a crease in his trail coat and just nicking his tricep.

Instinctively, he ducked low and reined his horse to the left. He pulled out his Winchester and jumped to the ground, making it look like he'd been hit badly. His horse bolted, ears pinned back and the whites of his eyes showing, but Ray wasn't worried; he knew that with a whistle, the horse would return.

Another shot rang out, kicking up spumes of sand three feet from where he lay. Ray rolled several times to his right, wincing every time his upper arm hit the dirt, but he knew he had to move. The shooter had a marker; the next shot might not miss.

The sun was showing its face just above the distant mountains to the east, and Ray knew that in ten minutes, the whole prairie would be lit up and he'd be a sitting target. He had to keep moving.

Two shots rang out, neither was anywhere near him but now he knew there were two of them out there and if he got caught in crossfire, he'd be doomed. Ray saw a brief flash as the rifles were fired so he got a bead on their position: a small outcrop that provided them with cover, he could only hope that one of them would make a mistake.

And one of them did.

Burt didn't like missing. He didn't like wasting bullets, either. He was lying prone on the smooth rock but he needed more height. It never entered his head that the sheriff was in a position to fire at him. Already they'd loosed off five shots without reply, so either the critter was dead, or badly wounded.

Burt decided to stand.

From Ray's position, a shooter was perfectly silhouetted against the early morning sky. Ray smiled and tucked the butt of the Winchester firmly under his right arm, and sighted down the long barrel. There was no wind to speak of, so he beaded in on the man and slowly, gently, squeezed the trigger.

8

'I'll get my foreman, Josh Kincaid in, I can trust him,' Lowe said, standing.

'No need for you to go, Ambrose, that's what Alfred is for. Alfred, please ask Mr Kincaid to join us.' Waring smiled sweetly, enjoying showing off his position.

'Yessir, Mr Waring, right away,' the ever eager Alfred replied and left the room.

'He's a good boy is Alfred,' Lowe remarked.

There was a knock at the door. 'Come in,' Waring shouted.

Josh Kincaid entered with a look of apprehension on his face, his Stetson held firmly in front of him.

'You may go, Alfred, I shan't be requiring you anymore this evening,' Waring said in a dismissive tone.

'Thank you, sir, Mr Waring. I'll be in

bright and early in the morning,' Alfred said, somewhat relieved to be getting out of the office.

'I'm sure you will, Alfred. I'm sure you will,' Waring said. To Josh he added, 'Take a seat, Mr Kincaid, we have a proposition for you.'

Kincaid relaxed somewhat and sank into one of the chairs.

'Drink?' Waring asked, holding the decanter out.

'Obliged,' Kincaid replied.

Waring waited while Kincaid drank his whiskey. Then, with a small cough, he placed his elbows on the desk and steepled his hands.

'We have a somewhat, er, delicate situation that we are hoping you might be able to solve for us. The risk is small, but the rewards are great.

'We have certain plans that have been jeopardized by the arrival of a certain, er, gentleman in town.' Waring stopped and waited for a response.

There was none.

Waring went on. 'You will, of course,

be suitably rewarded for your help in this matter.'

Kincaid picked up his empty shot glass and held it out.

Waring did his best to hide his annoyance at the arrogance shown by Kincaid. He topped up the glass and waited.

Then Kincaid spoke. 'What 'plans' would they be?'

'That is of no concern to you,' Waring stated firmly.

'You want me to kill somebody then it does concern me,' Kincaid said.

'Who mentioned killing? We merely wish you to make his stay in Bristow — short,' Clint said, speaking for the first time.

'An' who is this 'gentleman'?' Kincaid asked.

Waring glanced at Jenkins and Lowe before speaking.

'We're willing to pay $200 for your help,' the bank manager said.

'Who is he?' Kincaid asked again.

Again, Waring glanced at his partners before answering.

'Well, he could be a federal marshal.'

'What? Are you all crazy?' Kincaid couldn't believe his ears.

'Far from it,' Waring replied. 'There are millions of dollars at stake here and we can't afford to have a federal marshal poking his nose around.'

'You're talking about 'millions of dollars' an' you offer me two hundred?' Kincaid stood as if to leave.

'Wait,' Lowe said, also standing. 'I'm sure we can make a better offer, a much better offer.'

'You better come closer to 10,000,' Kincaid said.

'Ten thou — ' Waring began, a look of horror on his face.

'You heard right,' Kincaid said. 'The feds won't stop hunting for whoever 'runs off' one of their own. You know that as well as I do.'

The three businessmen looked at one another until Clint Jenkins nodded, as did Lowe.

Waring was open mouthed. 'We can't afford — '

'You wanna make millions? What's 10,000 in comparison?' Kincaid said.

Waring gave in. 'All right, all right. I agree to your demands. But I tell you this. You fail and you get nothing.'

'I want five up front or it's no deal,' Kincaid said. The steely look in his eye sent a shiver down Waring's spine.

'Agreed,' Lowe said. 'There's too much to lose here to quibble.'

★ ★ ★

The Winchester slug caught Burt in the fleshy part of his thigh. The impact sent him flying backwards and he toppled off his perch and fell ten feet to the ground. The sand was soft and cushioned his impact, but winded him so badly he was gasping for breath.

'Burt! Where are you hit?' Chad ran to his side.

'Damn critter . . . got me . . . in the leg.'

Chad took out his knife and cut into Burt's jeans to take a look at the wound.

'Not quite a flesh wound, but bullet's gone straight through. Ain't much bleedin', bro. I'll bind it up. Sure is gonna be sore for a while.'

'Tell me about it!' Burt spat.

The sun had sunk down behind the horizon and the scene was bathed in a faint blue glow from the moon in its last quarter. All this was to Ray's advantage.

He knew where the shooters were, and he guessed he knew *who* they were, but he had the added bonus of them not knowing where he was.

The pain in his shoulder had eased off and the bleeding had stopped; now, it was just uncomfortable. Crouching, Ray zigzagged closer to the outcrop. The eerie silence seemed to intensify and, as clouds scudded high in the black sky, blotting out the feeble light from the moon, the prairie was in total darkness for long periods of time.

There had been no return fire from the shooters and Ray wondered if he'd managed to kill or just wound one of them. Either way, the odds were getting more in his favour.

Lying flat on the ground, resting his elbows in the soft sand, Ray had the Winchester tucked firmly in his armpit. He sighted along the long barrel, waiting for any sign of movement.

Having bound Burt's leg tightly, Chad picked up his rifle and crawled to the side of the outcrop. It was too dark to see anything but he kept watch nevertheless.

'I'll skirt round to one side, you stay here. Any sign of movement, open fire. We might catch him in the crossfire,' Chad said.

'OK, I can manage to get to the other side of the rockface here. Let's nail the bastard,' Burt whispered.

Dragging his injured leg behind him, Burt made his way to the edge of the outcrop and positioned himself where, had it been light enough, he would have had a clear view. He strained his eyes, staring into the blackness of the night, trying to make out anything that shouldn't be there, but could see nothing.

Meanwhile, Chad had left the outcrop and was moving in an arc to Burt's left, hoping he'd not be seen by the sheriff. But fate took a hand.

Chad had gone no more than twenty yards when there was a break in the clouds and the feeble light from the moon silhouetted him perfectly.

Ray went for the legs. His shot was true and Chad fell to the ground, groaning.

'Chad, you OK?' Burt shouted, but there was no immediate reply.

'Chad!' he called again.

'Leg hit, bro,' came a faint reply.

'Toss out them weapons, boys. I'm taking you in!'

Ray's order was answered by a burst of erratic gunfire. It was clear the Slim brothers had no idea where he was as the slugs landed harmlessly way over to his right. But Ray now knew exactly where the brothers were; the muzzle flashes were a dead giveaway.

'I'll ask one more time,' Ray said. 'Throw down your guns, it's over. If I shoot again, it'll be to kill!'

More shots, but this time from only one rifle.

'I'm bleedin' bad, here, Burt,' Chad called out. 'I'm tossing my rifle and side iron, Sheriff.'

'You better go help your brother, Burt. He's likely to bleed to death if'n you don't,' Ray shouted. 'Just make sure you drop them guns. I see you carrying, I shoot. Got that?'

Burt didn't answer but Ray heard the clatter of metal on metal as Burt dropped his guns on the rocks. Standing, he raised his hands to show they were empty and made his way, limping, to his stricken brother.

Ray kept his rifle trained on him all the way.

As soon as Burt reached his brother, Ray stood, rifle at hip level, and started to walk towards them.

Burt had used his bandanna as a tourniquet to try and stop the bleeding in Chad's leg. Out of the corner of his eye, he saw the sheriff approaching. Suddenly, Burt lunged forward and made a grab for the Colt that Chad had discarded, but Ray was ready; he loosed off a shot that caught Burt in his gun hand, and his trigger finger took the full force of the.45–40.

Burt let out a scream that shattered the prairie peace. He clutched his hand and screamed again as he saw the index finger barely hanging on, only the tendons stopped it from hitting the dirt.

'Damn fool thing to do,' Ray said, emotionlessly, and tossed his own bandanna to Burt. 'You better wrap that hand up.'

Reaching into the back of his gun belt, Ray dragged out two sets of handcuffs. He threw one set to Chad and ordered him to put them on. The other set he roughly put on Burt.

'Now,' Ray said, 'we're gonna take a nice ride back to Bristow. You try anything and you're dead men. Savvy?'

Both men nodded morosely.

Ray gave a loud whistle and, in a matter of minutes, his mount returned.

'Now you help your brother to mount up and no funny business,' Ray said as he got on his horse. He put his rifle back in the scabbard and took out his Colt. 'I'm keeping you both covered. Remember that.'

* * *

The ride back to Rochester, though tedious, was uneventful and Ray was glad the local deputy sheriff agreed to lock them up for the rest of the night and get a doctor in to look at the men's wounds.

Ray took the horses to the livery and got them bedded down before going back to the sheriff's office. It was too late for either food or a bed for the night, so Ray had no alternative but to take a brief sleep in one of the vacant cells. The deputy produced coffee and a cookie jar. 'Best I can do, I'm afraid.'

'This is more than welcome,' Ray

thanked the man.

Fortunately his cell was out of sight of the Slim brothers. He sat on the cot, drained his coffee and ate a couple of the cookies before lying back and falling asleep almost instantly.

★ ★ ★

The sun had been up for nearly an hour when movement woke Ray from a deep sleep. Looming over him, holding a tray in both hands, was the sheriff.

'Figured you could do with breakfast,' the sheriff of Rochester said. 'Name's Art Derby. Deputy told me what gives here.'

'I'll be outa your hair shortly,' Ray said. 'Get these killers back to Bristow.'

'Well, the doc fixed their legs up some, an' amputated the trigger finger of one of them. Kicked up a fuss and my deputy had to — how shall I put it — send him to sleep for a while.' The sheriff grinned. 'Sure is a resourceful boy,' he added.

170

Sheriff Derby was relieved to hear that Ray and his two prisoners were leaving early. He liked a quiet life and let many things slide past both him and the law.

'I'll leave you to eat. I'll be in the office if'n you need anythin',' the sheriff said as he backed out of the cell.

'Thanks for the breakfast,' Ray said to the departing sheriff.

It didn't take Ray long to wolf down the breakfast and drain his coffee cup. He took the tray to the front office and put it on the sheriff's desk.

'Got the livery man to bring your horses round,' Derby said, 'they're on the hitch rail outside.'

'Thanks, Sheriff, and thanks for your hospitality. Guess I'll be heading off to Bristow now.'

'I'll get the prisoners.'

'Right behind you,' Ray said and the two men entered the cell block. Ray cuffed Chad first and then a grumbling Burt. 'Let's go, we got an eight hour ride ahead of us an' I ain't stopping.'

Both men limped out of the cell, Derby in front and Ray behind, his revolver drawn.

Between the two sheriffs, they managed to get the Slim brothers saddled up. Ray took his lariat and tied their horses together and tied the end to his pommel. Satisfied the killers were secure, he mounted up.

'Be seeing you, Sheriff and, once again, thanks for your hospitality.' Ray tipped his hat in a farewell gesture and the three left Rochester.

9

The weather had taken a turn for the worse. A strong wind, coming from the north, seemed to be bringing winter early. The sky had turned a dull grey, almost blotting out the sun completely. Sand was being whipped up and small dunes were already forming.

Hunched forward in their saddles, the three men tried to keep the sand and debris out of their eyes, as did their animals, but it was a futile job. The sand got everywhere eventually and the men felt as if their skin was being blasted.

'Hell, can't we find shelter and get out of this wind?' Burt yelled. His right hand was throbbing and he could swear he still felt his index finger, even though it was wrapped in a bandanna and tucked in his saddle-bag.

'No, there ain't no shelter till we hit

Bristow,' Ray replied.

'Where the hell is this sand coming from?' Chad yelled against the noise of the wind. 'All I can see is grass.'

'Wind picks it up and dumps it, comes from further north,' Ray replied and stopped his horse. Pulling the other two horses closer, he then tied bandannas over the two men's faces, covering their eyes, nose and mouth.

'You ain't got no reason to see an' this'll help keep your eyes clear of sand,' Ray said before digging his heels into the horse's flanks and continuing on southbound to Bristow at a trot.

It was four hours later when the three men reached the outskirts of Bristow. The wind had abated slightly and the stinging sand had come to a rest. Shopkeepers were out in force, brushing down the boardwalks and levelling out small dunes from Main Street.

Reining in at his office, or at least what had been his office, Ray stretched out his tired limbs, took his Stetson off and shook it to get rid of the trail dust and took his duster off and did the same thing.

He left the Slim brothers mounted and entered the office. Otis jumped to his feet and gave a broad smile.

'Good to see you, er, Sheriff.' He faltered.

'I see you got the job, Otis. Don't worry, I've come back with the Slim boys and I aim to take in Waring, Lowe and Jenkins.'

'Federal marshal is in town,' Otis said. 'I gave him the papers last night and he's planning on confronting Waring any minute now.'

'Where is he?' Ray asked.

'I jus' took him breakfast. He stayed in one of the cells last night.'

Ray took off his badge and put it on the desk. 'Guess I won't be needing this.'

Otis didn't know what to say, so he said nothing, just lowered his eyes to the floor.

'I got the Slim boys outside, you

might wanna bring them in and lock them up. They'll need help dismounting.'

Ray went through to the cell block to introduce himself to the marshal and to fill in the details of what he'd discovered.

Their conversation was, however, cut short as a gunshot shattered one of the front windows of the sheriff's office.

Ray and the marshal immediately drew their side irons and ducked through to the office.

Otis was standing at the front door, seemingly frozen.

'Get down, Otis!' Ray shouted.

After some hesitation, Otis dived to the floor and lay still.

Another shot rang out, thudding harmlessly into the woodwork surrounding the door.

'What the hell?' the marshal whispered.

'Beats me, but I think I'm the target,' Ray said.

'You sure about that? I don't think

me being here is welcomed,' the marshal said.

'I don't know who the shooter is, but I know who's behind it,' Ray said through gritted teeth.

'Waring and his cohorts?'

'Stake my life on it,' Ray replied. Then to Otis, he said, 'Get back here, Otis, you're too near the window there.'

Otis scrambled to the cell block door, keeping low. More shots rained in; glass and splintered wood shot through the air.

'There's more'n one of 'em,' the marshal declared. 'There a back door?'

'Yeah. Otis, stay in the cell block, you'll be safe there. I'm gonna get the rifles from the rack, cover me,' Ray said.

The marshal and Otis started to fire as Ray ducked down and reached a gun rack. Keeping as low as possible, he reached up, brought three Winchesters down and grabbed boxes of ammunition.

He slid the rifles across the floor, followed by the bullets. He then crawled back to the cell block.

Standing behind the cell door, he took a glance out through the shattered windows.

The Slim brothers had gone.

'Damn it to hell!' Ray uttered. 'They're gone. They won't get far, they each took a slug in the leg and they're cuffed. We'll concentrate on the shooters.

'You and me, Marshal, we'll split up. You to the left, me the right. You see any muzzle flashes, Otis?'

'Nary a one,' Otis replied, busily loading a Winchester. His eyes were bright with excitement and, Ray thought, a little fear.

'You keep your head down, Otis. On the count of three, you start firing, that should distract whoever is out there while we leave. OK? And by the way, don't shoot us,' Ray added with a grin. 'One . . . two . . . THREE!'

At the shout of three, Otis began firing as the two men dashed to the back door. Once outside, they split up and slowly made their way around the sheriff's office and towards Main Street.

The shooting stopped.

★ ★ ★

One dim lantern shone from the bank's front window.

In the manager's office sat three very nervous men. They flinched when the shooting started, and started to sweat when an eerie silence pervaded the town. Nervously, Waring lifted a decanter and poured its contents into three glasses, spilling some on his highly polished desk.

Lowe and Jenkins leaned forward, picked up a glass each and knocked the contents down in one gulp.

'It's too quiet,' Waring said, his voice quivering. 'We have no idea what's going on out there,' he added.

'Only one way to find out,' Jenkins said. 'We go take a looksee.'

'Are you crazy?' Lowe said. 'We're likely to get out heads shot off.'

'Nonsense,' Jenkins said. 'We're two blocks away from the sheriff's office. We can't just sit here and wait to see what the outcome is.'

'Clint's right. We'll go out of our minds just sitting here,' Waring agreed.

Jenkins took out his gun and checked its load, adding a sixth slug to the chamber.

'You intend on using that?' Lowe asked, a look of horror on his face.

'Ambrose, it's our men out there. How would it look if we just stood and stared like some yeller belly?'

Jenkins holstered his pistol and stood. 'Let's go. We need to get this finished, one way or another.'

* * *

Ray was at the corner of the sheriff's office and he hoped Sam Brown was on the opposite side.

He scanned Main Street, looking for any sign of movement or, at least, muzzle flashes. But the street was deserted, townsfolk hidden in their homes or businesses.

The silence was almost deafening, broken only by the whinnying of a horse. Ray looked to where the noise had come from and saw his two prisoners, still mounted, but their horses tied to a hitch rail outside the mercantile store. Neither man was able — or capable of — dismounting on their own.

He watched the two men, their heads bent low; all the fight and bravado had been drained from them. As he watched, he saw three figures approaching, keeping tight to the buildings.

'Well, well. They finally showed their hand,' Ray said to himself. He could see Clint Jenkins leading, Curtis Waring came next and lastly, Ambrose Lowe.

Jenkins had his pistol out.

Ray was distracted by a shot coming from the other side of Main Street. He saw the hat of the man who had fired; at last he had a position. From inside the sheriff's office, Otis loosed off a

181

couple of shots, but it was obvious Otis didn't have a bead on the man as the shots split wood way over to the man's left.

Ray tucked the Winchester tightly under his arm and sighted down the long barrel.

The man was behind a water trough outside a millinery store.

Ray aimed at the trough. With luck, the force of the .45–40 would go straight through.

Taking a deep breath and holding it, Ray gently squeezed the trigger, feeling the slight resistance just before the shell erupted from the barrel and winged its way towards its target.

In an explosion of wood and water, Ray heard the yelp and then short-lived scream as the bullet found its target.

Ray quickly cocked the rifle, ready for another shot. But there was no need: the man was either dead or badly wounded.

Sam heard the shot and the following yell and muttered, 'One down, how many more to go?' He sighted down his rifle, watching and waiting.

★ ★ ★

The three members of the town council inched their way forwards, halting as they heard the sound of gunfire, but the shots weren't aimed at them.

It was then that Jenkins saw the two mounted men. 'Isn't that the Slim boys?' Jenkins said.

'Damn!' Waring swore. 'If they talk, we're done for!'

'It also means Ray Cairney is back in town,' Lowe said.

'They ain't gonna talk,' Jenkins said in a harsh voice.

Moving closer and keeping tight against the livery building, Jenkins took aim with his pistol.

The Slim brothers, their heads still bowed and practically asleep, were totally unaware of the situation.

Jenkins pulled the trigger and Burt Slim's head exploded in a volcano of blood and gore.

Chad immediately sat bolt upright. He tried to heel his mount away as fast as possible, but the two animals were still tied together and Burt's horse was on its hind legs. It wasn't going anywhere.

Jenkins fired again; this time the slug buried itself deep in Chad Slim's chest, sending him flying backwards to land in the dirt.

'That's one problem solved,' Jenkins said, taking out the used shells and replacing them with fresh slugs. 'Now all we gotta do is get rid of Cairney and the federal marshal.'

Waring and Lowe were both speechless and horrified at what they had just witnessed. Neither man had seen this side of Jenkins before and suddenly they were even more afraid.

The two shots from Jenkins's pistol made Ray swing his head and rifle to his left. He watched as one of the Slim brothers flew through the air and even heard the thud as he hit dirt.

He saw Jenkins, his pistol still in his hand and smoke coiled from the barrel. *God damn*, he thought, *what the hell?*

But his attention was brought back to his own predicament as rifle shots started up again from across the street. Immediately Sam and Otis began to fire. The noise was deafening as whoever it was that was intent on killing him and the federal marshal, had taken heart and intensified their efforts.

Ray counted at least five shooters. At that point one of the shooters made a mistake.

Stationed on the roof opposite, he raised his head just a tad too high, and Ray took a shot and the man exploded. The rifle he was holding went flying down into the street, while the man himself was hurtled backwards to disappear from sight.

Another one down, Ray thought.

Sam had seen the man on the roof and shot at him almost the same time as Ray, but he was wide of the mark. A great volley of shots now erupted from the remaining shooters, but then suddenly stopped as quickly as it had started.

★ ★ ★

Josh Kincaid had decided a change of tactics was needed. The frontal assault, coupled with the element of surprise, hadn't worked.

'Clem, you and Jim-Bob circle round the back of the sheriff's office. Here,' he tossed a full box of vestas. 'Get what you can and torch the place, wood's tinder dry, should flush 'em out and we can pick 'em off.'

Clem and Jim-Bob knew exactly what to do. The lure of $100 each for their help was more than enough incentive.

They ran round the back of the buildings opposite the sheriff's office and then, two blocks down, emerged onto Main Street.

The street lanterns were within easy reach and, making sure they had oil in them, Clem grabbed one and Jim-Bob another. They crossed Main Street, unseen by either Ray or Sam, and made their way down the alleys that led to the rear of the sheriff's office.

Meanwhile, out front, Kincaid and the two men with him opened up with a barrage of random shots that kept Ray, Sam and Otis under cover, giving Clem and Jim-Bob time to set things up.

They reached the rear of the sheriff's office and Clem and Jim-Bob set the lanterns on the ground. Clem took out the Lucifers, struck one and lit both lanterns.

'OK,' Clem said, 'on the count of three!' They both swung the lanterns back and forth. 'One, two, three!'

Tossing them high in the air, both lanterns landed on the wooden shingles of the roof of the sheriff's office.

Inside, Otis heard the thump as they landed and kept his eye on the ceiling. The sound was too soft for it to be a person up there, but what the hell was it?

Burning oil ran down the tinder-dry shingles and within a few minutes, the roof was ablaze, sparks lifting into the air on the thermal.

Kincaid grinned as he watched the flames begin to engulf the building.

The townsfolk, who had been hiding in their homes and stores across the street, keeping their heads down, began to see the flames shoot skywards as the fire took hold.

There were very few stone buildings in Bristow, wood being readily available, and the worst nightmare of any small town was fire!

The gentle wind blowing in from the prairie was enough to fan the flames and pretty soon the buildings either side of the sheriff's office began to smoulder. If something wasn't done — and soon — the whole town could burn to the ground.

Waring, Lowe and Jenkins looked on in horror as they watched the fire hungrily devouring anything in its path.

Inside, the office was rapidly filling

with smoke and the building started to groan as the roof became unstable and the beams began to lick up the flames.

Otis kept as low as he could to avoid breathing in the smoke, but it soon became very clear that he had to get out, and that was what Kincaid was waiting for.

Ray was the first to react. Running to the rear of the building, he peered round the corner and saw two men watching the fire. Taking out his Colt, he took aim and fired twice in quick succession. He didn't care where the slugs went as long as they hit their target.

They did.

Clem and Jim-Bob didn't know what hit them as the slugs sent them careering backwards to land heavily in the alley.

Ray ran to the brick-built rear of the office where the cells were located and shouted through the bars. 'Otis, Otis, can you hear me?'

At first, there was no reply, but after

hearing coughing, Ray heard a faint reply. 'Here, Sheriff.'

'Come to the cell block,' Ray called, 'don't go out the front.'

Otis crawled and clawed his way to the rear of the building and appeared behind the bars of one of the cells.

Ray whistled and his horse, which was in the corral at the livery a block away and still saddled, pricked up his ears. He knew what the whistle meant. Leaping the corral fence with ease, the horse soon found his master.

Ray immediately took his lasso from the saddle horn and tied one end through the cell bars. He mounted up and tied the other end round the pommel as he guided the horse close to the burning building. His horse didn't shy away, although his ears were flat to his head and the whites of his eyes showed that he was none too keen on the idea but complied nonetheless.

Digging his heels in, Ray urged the animal into an instant gallop. The jolt of the rope nearly brought the saddle and

Ray off the horse, but after a second, the cell bars came crashing out to land in the alleyway.

Otis scrambled through, his face smoke-smeared and he lay on the ground, coughing and spitting.

Then he got to his hands and knees, the coughing stopped and he spat one final time. 'Sure thought I was a goner there, Sheriff.'

Behind him, the office roof collapsed, sending a shower of sparks high into the air. The ever-hungry flames sought new sources to burn. Otis stood unsteadily and moved further away from the inferno. To his surprise, he was still holding the Winchester in his right hand.

'Five more minutes and you woulda been, Otis. Either from the fire or from them shooters out front,' Ray said.

'I was ready to make a run for it,' Otis said. 'Better to die by a bullet than burn or choke to death.'

Sam appeared from the other side of the building. The smoke was thicker on his side and he was coughing and spluttering, bent at the waist, trying to clear his lungs. Eventually, he stood upright, spat and cleared his throat.

'That was pretty damn close,' was all he said as he took in the two dead men.

Ray dismounted and reached for his makings. As he built a cigarette he outlined his plan.

'Now them fellas out front will assume that, as Otis didn't come out, he was dead. This works to our advantage,' he said.

'How so?' Otis asked.

'For one, they didn't know who or how many were still in the office. Now, we split up. I want you, Otis, to stay on this side, just move one block down where you get a good view of Main Street. Sam and I will circle left and right and come on up behind them critters. They won't be expecting that, 'specially with Otis giving us covering fire.'

'That could work,' Sam agreed.

'I'm with you on this,' Otis said.

Further discussion was interrupted as the flames licked hungrily at the gun cabinet, the ammo overheated in the drawer and slugs were flying every which way. The three men instinctively ducked, but most of the exploding slugs shot straight into the air, those that didn't thudded harmlessly into the brick wall of the cell block, and a few peppered what was left of the timber-work at the front of the office.

The explosions stopped abruptly.

Standing, Ray said, 'OK, let's do this. Give us five minutes, Otis, then start shooting.'

Making sure both rifle and pistol were fully loaded, the three split up.

* * *

Waring and Lowe watched open mouthed as the flames began to spread. Jenkins stood impassively; all he could think about was making sure Cairney and the federal marshal were dead.

'We've got to do something about the fire,' Waring said. 'We can't let the town go up in flames!'

'Not much we can do about it,' Lowe said. 'Folks are too scared to venture out in case they get shot.'

'Damn fool Kincaid,' Jenkins said. 'Ain't got the sense of a racoon.'

'Kincaid! Hold your fire,' Waring shouted. 'We've got to put that fire out before it spreads too far.'

The shout was answered by the ammunition in the sheriff's office exploding, the smell of black powder almost overbearing. But Waring didn't know the cause of what he thought were shots from Kincaid.

'Seems like he ain't taking no notice,' Jenkins said.

'Kincaid, this is Ambrose Lowe. I order you to stop shooting!'

'Are you crazy?' Jenkins said. 'If the sheriff and the federal marshal aren't taken care of, you can forget about the railroad money. We'll all be in the state penitentiary — or hanged!'

'Hanged! They can't hang us, we haven't killed anyone,' Lowe said, aghast.

'We hired them two,' Jenkins replied, pointing at the dead Slim brothers.

'But they can't testify now,' Lowe insisted.

'No. But Cairney knows and has the proof that they 'visited' the Higgins' place and left a foreclosure note, signed by you, Waring.'

Waring stared at the ground.

'We've come too far to stop now,' Jenkins went on.

Grudgingly, Lowe and Waring had to agree.

* * *

Ray was in position now. He couldn't see Sam, but guessed he must be too.

Then the shooting started.

On the roof, immediately in front of Ray, he could see two men peering over the top towards the sheriff's office.

Ray took aim and fired. One man

went somersaulting over the apex of the roof. He didn't make a sound, but Ray heard the crunch as he landed in Main Street.

With all the shooting from Otis, the second man didn't notice until it was too late. He flung himself flat on the roof and Ray fired again, taking the top of the man's head clean off.

Kincaid saw the body of the first man as it landed in front of him. It twitched for a few seconds before lying still.

Damn! Kincaid knew at once that someone was behind him and his men. He hadn't seen hide nor hair of Clem and Jim-Bob, and they certainly hadn't been firing their weapons, so he feared the worst.

Seven against what he assumed to be two seemed good odds but now, Josh Kincaid was beginning to wish he'd never taken this job on — even for $10,000.

'Hop, you there?' Kincaid called out.

'Sure am, me an' Will,' came the reply.

'So there's just three of us,' Kincaid said absently

Which was exactly the thought that went through Ray Cairney's mind.

Suddenly, Ray tensed as he saw movement to his left, but relaxed when he saw it was Federal Marshal Sam Brown half crouching towards him.

'You hear that?' Ray said.

'Sure did. Evens the odds up a tad, I reckon,' Sam replied with a grin on his face.

'I saw Clint Jenkins take out the Slim brothers in cold blood. They were handcuffed and unarmed,' Ray said.

'They sure must want this mess covered up,' Brown said. 'That's why they want us rubbed out. Then there'd be no witnesses.'

'Well, they ain't gonna do it by hiring cowpokes to do their dirty work,' Ray said, loading his weapons.

Two shots rang out, shattering the silence, but they weren't aimed at the two lawmen.

'We better help Otis out,' Ray said.

'Let's check out the back door there,' Sam said and began to edge forward. Ray followed.

On reaching the door, Sam tried the handle. The door was not locked and, crouching low, they entered the building.

It took a while for their eyes to adjust to the gloom, but when they had, both men could see a long corridor. There were holes in the side walls where slugs had penetrated and each hole had a shaft of bright light illuminating the dust specks that hung in the air.

At the end of the corridor there was a door, also bullet-riddled, and halfway down there were two more doors; one to the left and one to the right.

Ray pointed at Sam, then the left-hand door. Then he pointed at himself and the right-hand door. Sam nodded that he understood.

Quietly, the two men moved forward until they reached the doors. Ray held up three fingers and one by one lowered them. Both men turned the

door handles at the same time and
burst into each room.

10

'It seems, gentlemen, that we have to finish the job ourselves,' Jenkins said. 'I suggest you draw your weapons. Let's get this done!'

'May I remind you, Clint, we are not gunfighters. I've never even fired a gun at a person and I'm damn sure I couldn't,' Waring said.

'I've shot rustlers,' Lowe admitted, 'but that's the law of the land. That and hangin' 'em. But shooting lawmen? I can't be doing that.'

'If we don't get rid of them lawmen, the whole scheme dies. Is that what you want? Right this minute the foreclosure notices are being delivered, and in less than a week we'll be the richest men in the county, and with money, comes power. Can't you see that?' Jenkins stared at the two men, his eyes burning black.

It was Lowe who spoke, slowly, and methodically. 'I guess you're right, Clint. We've come too far to stop now and, much as it goes against the grain, you're right.'

Waring was a bag of nerves. His hands shook and sweat was running down his now bright red face.

'What d'you say, Curtis?' Jenkins asked. 'Are you with us or agenst us?'

'Guess I have no choice. It's my signature on those notices, my reputation on the line.'

'If we fail, you won't have a reputation to worry about,' Lowe stated.

'OK, let's go find Kincaid,' Jenkins said.

★   ★   ★

It was the federal marshal who drew the short straw.

As he burst into the room off the corridor, he was confronted by the man known as Hop. He drew, albeit clumsily, but still got a shot off before Sam Brown could respond. The slug caught Brown in the right arm, shattering bone and sending the marshal spinning backwards, his right arm hanging uselessly by his side.

Hop was about to finish the job when Ray entered and fired.

Hop took the full impact of the bullet in his chest and he went crashing through what was left of the store's front window, to land heavily on the boardwalk. Dead.

'You OK, Sam?' Ray asked.

'Gun arm. Bone's broken,' came a weak reply.

Quickly, Ray took off his bandanna and tied it tightly around the top of Sam's arm. He managed to stop the bleeding, which was a good sign. Then he took off the marshal's bandanna and made a sling to keep the arm still.

'You stay here. As soon as I've finished, I'll rustle up the doc and he can finish the job. Reckon you can shoot with your left hand?'

'Just put my gun in it,' Sam replied. 'I'll manage, you just take care out there.'

Ray managed to prop the marshal against an inner wall, who groaned some as he was moved, but once settled, it was more comfortable. Ray checked the Colt; it was fully loaded, so he handed it to the marshal.

'It's cocked and ready to fire,' Ray said.

'So am I,' the marshal replied, drily.

'By my reckoning, there's only two of 'em left — '

Ray was cut short by a shot and a man screaming briefly, then silence. Ray drew his own Colt and, keeping low, moved to the shattered window.

Across the street he saw Otis, his rifle still smoking and in the middle of Main Street, there was a body.

'Make that one,' Ray said to the marshal.

'Go get 'im,' Sam said through gritted teeth. The shock was beginning to wear off and the pain in his arm was starting to really hurt.

'I'll be back,' Ray said and left the room.

★   ★   ★

'Hop? Will?' It was Kincaid who called out, but there was no reply. He knew now he was on his own, it was kill or be killed.

Kincaid had stationed himself in a saddlery, next to the mercantile store that Ray and the marshal had entered. Across the street he briefly caught sight of Otis before he disappeared again in the swirling smoke.

The breeze had virtually stopped and the fire seemed content to devour the three buildings in its grasp and was slowly burning itself out.

Kincaid had heard two shots: the first he thought came from the mercantile store, the second he knew was from across the street. Then he caught sight of the body lying in the dirt in the middle of Main Street.

The body still wore the distinctive brown bowler that Will always wore.

'Damn!' Kincaid said under his breath.

He still had a choice. He could stay and take his chances against the three lawmen, or he could just walk away. He had plenty of money, more than enough to live the high life and what could Waring do about it? Nothing, that's what. In the end, it was an easy choice.

Ride!

Kincaid holstered his side iron and snuck out the back of the saddlery. His piebald horse was still hitched to a pole fence at the rear and he wasted no time in mounting up and disappeared in a cloud of dust.

Ray had heard the hoofs thudding on the hard packed dirt, but was too late to do anything about it. He knew, from the horse, who was riding out of town.

But it wasn't over yet. Two shots rang out, wild, erratic shots and Ray spun and ducked down. He holstered his

Colt and brought the Winchester to play.

Peering over the tall grass that covered the wasteland behind the mercantile, he saw three men. He recognized them immediately. So, they've thrown caution to the wind, he thought.

It was Jenkins who led the trio, and it was Jenkins who fired again. The other two had pistols drawn but hadn't fired — yet.

Ray sighted down the long barrel; he had Jenkins in his sight and was ready to pull the trigger. Then, out of the blue, a voice commanded, 'Hold it right there, gentlemen. One false move and you're dead.'

'Well, I'll be a — ' Ray looked on in wonder. There was Otis, rifle in hand and the three town council members caught red-handed.

'Drop them guns, now!' Otis said.

Waring and Lowe did so immediately, but Jenkins hesitated, then turned swiftly.

Ray didn't falter. He fired, low, he didn't want this man to die quickly, so he aimed for the legs and his shot was true.

Jenkins was flung to the ground, his pistol fired harmlessly into thin air. 'You goddamned cowards,' he mouthed at Waring and Lowe. 'Goddamn cowards!'

Epilogue

It would be another two months before the circuit judge arrived in Bristow. In the meantime, the three prisoners were kept in an unused storage room at the back of the mercantile store.

The sheriff's office and the two buildings either side of it had been rebuilt in record time and the prisoners moved into the new cells.

A new town council had been elected and Waring, Lowe and Jenkins were awaiting trial with some trepidation.

The circuit judge, Judge Abraham Walters was known to be a hard man with criminals — especially killers — and he wasted no time on formalities. He ate in the saloon while it was being turned into a courtroom as the Silver Dollar had the only room big enough to accommodate the townsfolk. The homesteaders, farmers and ranchers who had been served notice to quit were there in force as was the new bank manager, whose first task was to cancel the foreclosure notices.

Sam Brown had recovered fully, the doctor having worked miracles on the broken arm. He'd also attended to Jenkins's leg, although he had to admit to himself that he wasn't as gentle as he had been with the marshal.

Ethan Doom had had a field day, as the funerals were all paid for by the town council who recouped the money from the bank accounts of Waring, Lowe and Jenkins.

Judge Williams studied the documents before him and listened to the testimony of ex-Sheriff Cairney as well as that of Federal Marshal Brown.

He instructed the jury that there was only one outcome. They should talk amongst themselves to decide the fate of the three defendants, but they'd better come up with a guilty verdict. The deliberations took less than five minutes as the jury returned to their seats.

'Gentlemen, have you reached a verdict?' the judge asked.

Leonard Sumner, the foreman of the jury, stood up. 'We have, your Honour,' he stated firmly.

'And is it the verdict of you all?'

'It is, your Honour,' replied the foreman.

'In the matter of attempted fraud and intimidation, how do you find?'

'Guilty.'

'In the matter of accessory to the killing of six people, how do you find?'

'Guilty.'

'In the matter of the cold-blooded killing of the Slim brothers, how do you find?'

'Guilty, your Honour,' the foreman said, and sat down.

The acting court clerk stood up. 'The prisoners will stand,' he ordered.

'You have all been found guilty of the charges brought against you,' the judge began. 'A most heinous and despicable attempt to defraud good people from land that is rightfully theirs and to authorize the killing of one Swampy and one William Lancaster. For that, you, Waring and Lowe, are sentenced to life imprisonment with hard labour at the state penitentiary.

'You, Clint Jenkins, have been found guilty of the murder of two men in cold blood. Albeit they were also killers responsible for the murders mentioned, and as such, I sentence you to be hanged by the neck until dead.'

The judge stood.

'All rise,' the clerk ordered.

'This session is complete,' the judge said and banged his gavel.

A spontaneous cheer went up from the onlookers as the three guilty men were led away and Ray breathed a sigh of relief. Finally, it was over.

The town council thanked Ray and Sam and Otis for bringing law and order back to Bristow and even offered the job of sheriff to Ray.

He declined. 'You got a fine sheriff

already here in Otis, he did a fine job,' he said and Otis beamed, his face reddening at the same time.

Sam Brown tipped his hat and said his farewells; he wasn't a man to drag things out, and he rode back to the county seat. The township of Bristow got on with its life.

Ray walked Otis back to the new sheriff's office. 'What are you planning on doing now, Sheriff?' Otis asked.

'Otis, you're the sheriff, not me. I got a rendezvous with a certain lady that can't wait any longer.' Ray smiled.

'You dog,' Otis said. 'Anyone I know?'

'Nope.'

Ray packed his gear and shook Otis by the hand. 'You'll be a fine sheriff, Sheriff,' Ray said and left the office.

* * *

Two hours later, Ray rode up to the small ranch house and was greeted in the same way as his first visit. Sue, gun in hand, ordered him to stop and state his business.

Ray dismounted, took off his Stetson and said, 'Was wondering if you had a mind to hiring?'

Sue dropped the rifle she was holding and rushed towards him, stopping short of throwing her arms around his neck.

She blushed deeply. 'I — I didn't think I'd see you again,' she said.

Ray stepped forward, placed a finger under her chin, lifting her face to his.

Then they kissed.

Now it really was over.

We do hope that you have enjoyed reading this large print book.

Did you know that all of our titles are available for purchase?

We publish a wide range of high quality large print books including:
Romances, Mysteries, Classics
General Fiction
Non Fiction and Westerns

Special interest titles available in large print are:
The Little Oxford Dictionary
Music Book, Song Book
Hymn Book, Service Book

Also available from us courtesy of Oxford University Press:
Young Readers' Dictionary
(large print edition)
Young Readers' Thesaurus
(large print edition)

For further information or a free brochure, please contact us at:
Ulverscroft Large Print Books Ltd.,
The Green, Bradgate Road, Anstey,
Leicester, LE7 7FU, England.
Tel: (00 44) **0116 236 4325**
Fax: (00 44) **0116 234 0205**